This story is a work of fiction. Names, characters, places, and incidents are fictitious and any similarities to actual persons, locations, or events is coincidental. This work cannot be used to train artificial intelligence programs.

No AI tools were used in the writing of this book or to produce the artwork thereon.

ISBN: 978-1-998763-43-6

All rights reserved.

CHASERS © Mariah Darling, 2025
CHASERS © Eve Harms, 2025
Art and logos included in/on this volume © Unnerving, 2025

"With their debut collaboration, *Chasers*, Eve Harms and Mariah Darling bring the reader along for a wild and deeply felt ride. An unsettling mystery peopled with characters who instantly appeal, *Chasers* is propulsively plotted with a jaw dropping but all too believable premise. More than simply horror or thriller, the writing is accessible and enthralling. Would love to see more from this talented duo."

Laurel Hightower, author of *Crossroads* and *Every Woman Knows This*

"*Chasers* ratchets the tension by degrees until you're trapped in a depraved psycho-sexual nightmare. Gets its claws in you and won't let go! I loved it!"

Bitter Karella, author of *Midnight Pals* and *Moonflow*

"A tightly-wound rollercoaster ride about the dangerous realities of perception and desire for trans women. Unnerving from start to finish, Darling and Harms deliver a harrowing suspense story that will keep you up at night long after it's done. Brutal and necessary—Darling and Harms do not miss."

Magen Cubed, author of *Southern Gothic*

"Part Hitchcock, part Henenlotter, *Chasers* will make you shudder and squirm, sometimes all at once! Mariah Darling and Eve Harms have a bright future in horror fiction. I'm here for whatever either of them do next."

Lucas Mangum, Splatterpunk Award winning author of *Snow Angels* and *Saint Sadist*

CHASERS

MARIAH DARLING
EVE HARMS

To Shane, so great to hang out and chat books!! ♡ ♡

— Eve H

CHAPTER 1

I lift myself up onto the makeshift raft, nearly choking to death on the copper flavored liquid that spills out of my throat. It's a pitch black night, no stars or moon, but I can still see the bodies of dead trans women covering the surface of the crimson ocean. They float face up and face down, still so stunning even at rest, the bright colors of their editorial fashion mute under the red film of blood. Our blood.

I trip and scream, snapping back to reality, and grip the box of retro vases—I'm about to bust my ass on the steps of my old apartment building. I must have spaced out and remembered the nightmare that woke me up in a sweat—way too early this morning. I can be a little superstitious but not stupid enough to think that every weird dream I have has any meaning whatsoever. The last thing I need is a twisted ankle during my move. I recover (flawlessly), pull my little black purse back up on my shoulder, and peek inside the box to make sure nothing's chipped while I walk over to Max's double-parked van in my modest three-inch heels.

"Jesus, I don't think it's going to fit." Max wipes their sweaty brow, looking down at my box of tangled hair extensions that lean on the bumper. They've undone their red and black flannel shirt, letting it hang loose on their shoulders, revealing their lightly tanned skin and white tank top underneath.

"But I need my hair extensions," I say, panicking only slightly.

Max shrugs and gestures to the van completely stuffed with my things. They're an unintentional stud type—beautiful and androgynous.

They've never adopted a label (which I admire) but if I had to give them one it would be queer, for sure. They have a seductive charm—I've never seen them give a man the time of day, but they've always got some poor barbie drooling over them.

"I'm dying, if I have to carry one more box I will literally die. I will literally die, Lenora," Kierra says, bent over dramatically and panting with her arms carrying my box like a sling.

"That's literally the last box, girl." I reply. "You're not going to die. Dead girls can't eat pizza."

When she's not acting like a dramatic princess, Kierra pulls off that relaxed yet confident vibe. She looks a little like Lindsay Lohan but dresses like Courtney Love. I always give her snaps for her fashion efforts, because on most girls in this city it would look forced. There are so many posers here—authenticity is lacking—so when I see legit aesthetics I appreciate it. Kierra has long red hair (layered with choppy bangs), she's skinny, and sports a rack I'd kill for. She does nothing but complain about her gorgeous body, and I'm convinced that she pretends to be insecure so girls won't hate her. She's got her share of haters, so I'm not sure if that's working for her.

Speaking of haters, my ex-roommate Kat bursts out of the front door. Accidentally summoning her was the last thing I wanted; things are sour between us and I'd been avoiding her for a week, hoping we'd get my things out today before she woke up. "Where's the rest of the rent, bitch?"

I hand my box to Max, flip my hair back over my shoulder, and give her an accusing gesture with my bright red acrylics. "I gave my thirty-day notice, I'm not paying rent for two weeks that I'm not even living here."

"That was before you tried to steal my man, shit's

real different now, give me the keys, give me the money."

"YOU two propositioned ME. So, I didn't want to play sex doll in your little threesome fantasy with your dusty ass and your ugly man—not my fault if he's still obsessed with me. Be an adult and deal with it." I hear Max snicker at me reading her for filth and I hold back a smirk. Things are heating up, so I lower my right hand and quietly snap it a couple times. Max and Kierra get my signal and rush to finish loading the boxes.

"Ugly man? Look who's talking," Kat says before she lifts her head up and spits at me. That's practically assault.

She's lucky I'm a pacifist, or I'd already be taking off my earrings. Max's hand on my arm tells me the van is ready, so I pull out my old house keys (with the full-size troll doll keychain) and chuck it. The troll face-plants on the roof with the keys, making a satisfying plop and jingle. "That's all you're getting from me!"

I leave Kat screaming her head off, hurling vulgar words left and right, and jump in Max's van. As soon as my ass is in the seat, Max drives off like they're trying to lose the cops, leaving behind the chaos of my last living situation for good.

Never live with a couple! They ended up being creepy as hell. Kat and fucking Ronald. Not Ron,

Ronald. Gag me with a spoon. Plus, that place was moldy as hell, I can't believe I willingly lived like that.

It's not a long drive, we get off the 110 (god, it's so rundown) and navigate the little-maze of one-ways before going through the long tube tunnel under the stretch of freeway that cuts through downtown LA. We arrive at my new home, it's on the outskirts of downtown and walking distance from the metro. Plenty of action but a little bit tucked away. The architecture isn't like the LA apartments I'm used to: two stories of stucco with outdoor staircases, and catwalks to the units made of metal and concrete slabs embedded with stones. Instead, it's six stories with a New York vibe that I love. The outside is a beautiful brick facade, and it has those classic metal fire escapes. Green ivy is tastefully gracing the brick, and it even has its original neon sign from when it was a hotel named The Playhouse.

I hop out of the van while Max takes boxes off of Kierra (they had to stack a few on top of her to fit everything in). Soon the three of us are on the curb, admiring my new digs. Max crosses their arms and exhales from their nose in approval. "Nice place!"

Kierra goes "Wooowwwwww."

My smile is so big it warms my face. This is it, my new home. "Thanks so much for your help, babes, I really appreciate it. Should we get started?"

Kierra blocks me with her arm. "Wait. We gotta take a shot."

"We do?" Max says.

"Yea. Mom always said it's good luck to take a shot before you move into a new apartment—and bad luck if you don't." She looks deadly serious.

Kierra's mom was an alcoholic and died last year because of it, so this is weirdly sad. Her daughter didn't exactly follow in her footsteps, but she's a certified lush for sure. I'm not really a drinker (I prefer more herbal refreshments), but honestly after all the drama, maybe the liquor will help with the stress of the move. "What're we drinking?"

"Tah-kill-ya!" Kierra says in a horrible attempt at a British accent. She takes out a flask and three shot glasses from her little overstuffed purse. Always prepared.

Max cackles. "Okay, okay. To the new apartment, then."

We clink glasses. This is a moment worth celebrating. This apartment is going to change everything, it's the start of a new era.

As soon as I walked into the empty unit for the first time, I knew it had to be mine. I filled out my application on the spot and started picturing my furniture in the space, already mentally moving in while the manager looked it over.

My purple couch would go against the wall that was shared with the kitchen, and I'd put my big yellow shag carpet in front of it. The living room was spacious enough that we could easily have band practice there. Totally Toxic was on the verge of breaking out. I could feel it, Max could feel it, and even Kierra, who could be a bit of a space cadet, could feel it. We were close. But we needed more time to practice, and I needed more time and headspace to write new songs. This apartment is the key to both of those things.

We're only able to practice twice a month because that's all we can afford in the shared space we rent in Chinatown. Kierra's drum set wouldn't fit here, but her drum pad would do. And setting up my keyboard and Max's bass would be a cinch.

At first, I didn't think I'd get the place. I'd already lost out on a few apartments and the manager was a little hard to read—and kind of hot if I'm being honest. When he was looking over my application with a himbo squint he lifted his arm to rub his nose, and I got a glimpse of his large tan bicep sliding out of his red polo. The way it had flexed with the casual motion set me off a little. He definitely didn't skip the gym—he was ripped. He could probably pick me up. I guess I have a bit of a weakness for muscular, vaguely Italian-looking guys with black hair. I guess I have a bit of a weakness for a lot of different types of guys. He was well groomed too; you could tell that he took care of himself. A little older than me, but it wouldn't be weird, you know?

He took a while with my application, and I began to wonder if there was something wrong or if he was just a slow reader. Then he looked up at me with warm brown eyes, and I was struck by the confident eye contact. I swallowed and he deepened his gaze and said those nine words every woman wants to hear. "I just need to check your credit and references."

There were two problems with that—and I felt them in the pit of my stomach. First, my credit wasn't great (I think I technically didn't qualify for the apartment). It was decent before, but I had recently changed my name which caused it to drop 200 points through some weird (transphobic, if we're being honest) quirk of the credit score algorithm.

The second was my references. I couldn't give him the phone number for my boss at the boutique, because I quit a month ago. My photoshopped paystubs said I was still working at the shop and earning commissions, and that wouldn't have checked out if he talked to her.

And besides, the owner—my former boss—was weird. We were convinced her vaguely European accent was as fake as the meaningless name of the store, and she would go on and on about how "exotic" I was. One time she told me I looked like a llama. I know it was supposed to be a compliment, but it made me uncomfortable. Like, has she never seen a black trans woman before? She'd lived in the city long enough that she didn't have an excuse.

I'm not a pet. I'm not an "exotic creature," I'm not a fucking unicorn. I'm just a girl.

But she was mostly harmless, and she was definitely good for a laugh between me and Max and Kierra. Max had developed a magnificent impression of her that cracks us up. So that's who the apartment manager called instead of my real boss. They pulled it off beautifully. No surprise, I swear they were an actor in their past life. I overheard and they were giving a really juicy performance—I had to stop myself from laughing.

Kierra played the part of my ex-housemate Kat, she managed to avoid getting creative with the role and pulled it off too. Kierra is a killer drummer and social media wiz, but she's a terrible liar, so I told her to keep it dead simple. I figured at the very least she wouldn't slander me with accusations of being a homewrecker and deadbeat like the real Kat.

When the manager (his name is Ryan) went to check my credit, a giant number—"598"—surrounded by a red semi-circle popped up on the screen and he made a "hooo" sound to express his mild surprise and disappointment. Ryan told me that my score was too low, so I explained about my name change, hopefully without giving information that would clock me. You never know, he might have some ideas about trans people, and I didn't need to give him any reasons to deny me the apartment. It's caused me issues in the past. I was even refused hotel rooms because they assumed I was a prostitute.

About three-quarters of the guys I meet can't tell, so I wasn't sure if he was figuring out my status when I was explaining the name change situation or if his head was completely empty. Either way, he told me he would make an exception about my lousy credit score, and I got the place! Although, I had to ask myself: what's the catch? One thing I've learned in my journey of womanhood is that men never do something nice for you, just to be nice. Oftentimes they're expecting something in return. The last thing I wanted was to be indebted to a man.

But this apartment is perfect: affordable with (almost) new floors, new countertops, A/C units, and a dishwasher. It's spacious and doesn't have an awkward layout. It's quite charming, the bathroom has a clawfoot tub with stylish decorative tile on the wall behind it.

They even allow pets, maybe I could finally get a kitty, once I'm settled.

Such a refreshing change from the other decrepit apartments I'd seen that month with slumlords who charged hundreds more for cracked walls and painted-over kitchen tile and painted-over windowpanes.

Plus, it was all mine—no unstable or alcoholic roommates, or "artists" that take over the common areas with their weird sculptures, because they're too broke to get a studio space. Or creepy couples like Kat and Ronald. Sure, the rent in the new place is (much) higher, but it's a really good price for the area. The building is still being renovated, so the early tenants are getting a deal on rent. With all of the greedy landlords in this city, paying more is the only way to get out of a shitty situation.

I've finally found sanctuary. A place to heal. A place to grow. A place to take Totally Toxic to the next level. It's time to move on from the bullshit and move into my new, beautiful apartment. Number 202.

I take the shot of tequila with Max and Kierra and feel warm from the dark liquor settling on my chest with a slight burn. It does help with the stress. With Kierra's twisted family ritual out of the way, we snap a selfie for our band's Instagram. We take the first few boxes up the stairs, passing the charming grid of numbered, metal mailboxes and the tiny out-of-order elevator behind the beige door with a small plastic window. My unit is on the second floor. As we walk down the hall and approach my new apartment, I see Ryan closing the door and getting out a big, full keyring to lock up. He notices me and puts it on his belt instead. "Oh, hi, Lenora! Welcome to The Playhouse."

I haven't moved in yet, but it does feel a little weird that he was just in my apartment. "Hey, thanks, but um...what're you doing here?"

"Oh, just some last-minute repairs I had on my list before you moved in. Sorry, I know your move in date is today, I'm not usually a procrastinator...but it's all yours now."

He gives a half-grin like he told a joke; I doubt he's capable of forming a real one. But his smile is charming and melts away my worries about him coming into the apartment without giving notice. I mean, it's true that I don't live there yet.

And Kierra definitely likes him, she watches him walk all the way out, the ring of keys chiming as he does. I make a mental note to dish about him with Kierra later when Max isn't around.

There was this moment, when I was looking over the lease on the kitchen counter and he was explaining the different parts of it and showing me where to sign and initial. He was close, and I could smell his cologne and feel the heat of his body. I flushed, my heart sped up, and I pushed down a familiar feeling of sensual excitement. It made it a little hard to concentrate on the legalese of the lease, but it seemed pretty standard.

It's weird that I found him coming out of my apartment, but it also makes me feel kind of safe. Ryan cares about the unit, unlike previous managers who wouldn't even fix leaks. He's clearly proud of the building based on his bragging about how it used to be a historical hotel and has a "presidential suite" that he's converting into units. Having a diligent apartment manager is a good thing. I'm just not used to it.

After a few hours of bringing in boxes, and a ton of sarcastic comments from Max about how many clothes I have, we manage to get all of my things into the unit. I order pizza and beer from a delivery app to celebrate and thank my bandmate-besties. We lay out my fuzzy yellow shag rug and move my purple couch to the wall. I plop down on it and make an open gesture. "Our new practice space."

Max joins me on the couch. Kierra lies down on the rug and stares at the ceiling. "It's perfect."

My practice keyboard is poking out of a box within reach, so I pull it out, find a synth preset I'm drawn to, and start improvising. Playing hasn't come so easy in years. Fresh lyrics flow out of me. "These bitches are frauds, these bitches aren't loyal, whatever happened to sisterhood, where is the love?"

Max adds their a capella rendition of a baseline through a rolled up poster while Kierra beatboxes. She's actually pretty good. A smile spreads across my face and my singing becomes more passionate as I build up my chord progression. "Kat, I hope you heal, I hope you find peace, I hope you find happiness, and stop being a cunt!"

Max stops their bassline. "This is sick, Lenora. We've got something here."

The pizza and beer arrive. We continue to work on the song, letting the alcohol loosen up our creativity even more. Kierra sets up an impromptu drum set with boxes and cookware, and Max nuzzles up to me to play their bass line on the low end of my keyboard.

Kierra scrambles to her feet after a few minutes to set up her phone on a stack of boxes with the portable tripod she carries everywhere. "We gotta live stream this. Our fans are gonna freak over it."

We're so in sync, like we've played this song a hundred times, not like we were making it up as we went along. The view count climbs and hearts rise from the bottom of the phone's screen as I sing. "Fuck you bitch, just leave me alone. Just leave me alone. Fuck you bitch, because I'm home. I'm finally home."

    We laugh and cuddle and play and pass out in the living room without unpacking anymore; they're too drunk to drive; I'm too drunk to set up my bed. We leave the livestream on, so people will stumble upon us on their *For You* feed while we're sleeping. Kierra says it's an easy way to get followers, and I'm too wiped to care that it's kind of weird. Let them watch me sleep. Nothing can fuck this up.

CHAPTER 2

Angel opens the door and hurries me in with a nervous (and somehow cute) smile. He's already high, wearing a baggy plain white t-shirt and jeans and a silver chain around his neck with a small Jesus cross. I say a quick hi to his roommate and roommate's girlfriend on the way to his bedroom. He pulls me on to his ratty green couch and starts kissing up my neck. I push him away. "Aren't you even gonna put on a movie?"

He stares at me blankly. When I first hooked up with Angel, it was after a Totally Toxic show. He was hot and told me I was beautiful, and I thought he liked me because I was in a band, but it quickly became clear that he was after something else. He didn't want to take me on proper dates, he just wanted me to come over and fuck him. In the beginning we had at least a short conversation, and he'd put on a movie before we started, but he's apparently completely done with pretense.

He nods, "Yeah, sure," and tosses me the remote. I flip through the various movies and shows I've already seen or never heard of on his smart TV, and he loads his tall neon-plastic tube bong. After taking a large hit he hands it to me. I don't prefer it, a classy pink joint is more my style, but I don't turn it down. I take a dainty puff (I'm not rude), and I hand it back to him. And then he takes another, and another. What's wrong with him? How high does he have to be?

"You're smoking a lot, babe."

He looks at me, deadly serious, almost sad, and says, "I just need it to chill out. Or I feel like what we're doing is wrong."

I knew he was insecure, but this was on another level. The sex is pretty good but it's not worth dealing with his damage around being attracted to me. Attracted to my trans body. I want a man who knows who he is, secure and sure of himself. Not some coward chaser who can't even sit with himself without getting high. He'd never make me his girlfriend anyway; the relationship is going nowhere. I grab my bag and stand up, my head swimming just a touch. I have to steady myself. This is why I hate bongs. "I'm out."

"Wait, you can't leave."

"Like hell I can't."

He whines like a child, his hands wrapped around the neck of his bong, "I'm just being honest with you, you can't be mad at that."

"Try being honest with yourself." I slam his bedroom door behind me and stomp out of his apartment and try not to cry on the bus ride home. He's dead to me.

I'm uneasy as I step off the bus and walk home. The sidewalks overflow with debris, and I stumble past the tents and folding chairs of a homeless camp as I near my apartment. It's the first time I've seen my place from the outside at night and it's giving me the creeps. Does the fact that it's a full moon mean anything? Is something in retrograde right now?

The moon colors the building a cold blue and stark shadows speckle it. The boarded-up windows of the top floor (the presidential suite) look sinister and stand out; Ryan said it was already like that and that he'll replace them completely at some point. Does "presidential suite" mean that a president has stayed here before? Kind of a creepy thought, but I doubt it. I'm disoriented, and still baked from earlier.

The Playhouse's architecture is such a contrast to the standard LA complex that it doesn't even feel like I'm in the same city anymore. The red door and half-lit neon sign look both alien and familiar. Was this in a movie? Is it even real? I grab my pepper spray gel from the purse and hold it in my hand with my finger on the trigger and cross the street toward my new home.

Did a woman just come out of the bushes in the front? No, she must have walked out of a shadow. I can only see her from the back, she's wearing a blue clubbing dress with a shiny wide black belt and has on wedge gladiator sandals over her fishnets—these fashion influencers are unhinged. Her jet black hair is a complete mess and she's stumbling too. She must be really drunk the way she's struggling with that key.

She manages to get the door open and slams it behind her right away. But I caught a better glimpse of her. Was she a little clocky or did I imagine it? Her shoulders are wide, and she's got a squarish angle to her jaw; is she another trans woman? Or just a cis woman with broad shoulders and a strong jaw? Wait, am I being transphobic? I know plenty of cis women who pass for trans. Maybe it's just the light.

I unlock the front door, walk up the stairs, and turn into the hallway to my apartment. She goes into apartment number 203, which is right after mine, on the same side of the hall. I call out, but she slams the door behind her. She didn't hear me, I guess.

It's so quiet after that loud slam—and that broken flickering light down the hall—it's tripping me out. Is the building this dead quiet every night? Not that I'm complaining. But I hope I haven't become the noisy neighbor considering last night's band practice.

When I open the door to my apartment, I notice the light above the stove is on, peeking out from behind the wall that obscures the otherwise open kitchen. I don't think I've ever turned that on. There's movement, someone's behind that wall. My stomach tightens and eyes widen, un-focusing my vision.

I can't believe there's a break-in on my second night! Is it a burglar or pervert? Is it Ryan, the manager, *"fixing"* my refrigerator? It sounds like they're going through my kitchen cabinets.

I put my finger on the trigger of my pepper gel and walk toward the kitchen as quietly as possible. I'll take advantage of the element of surprise. After a deep breath, I jump out from behind the wall and pull the trigger on the kitchen invader. "Eat spice, bitch!"

It's Kierra. She screams with surprise, shaking the open box of hemp-superfood granola in her hand, causing it to explode all over the floor. Luckily, the pepper gel is expired or defective, and the blue goo just dribbles out. She screams a second time, shaking the box again, getting even more onto the floor and into unpacked boxes, which is completely unnecessary because she must recognize me by now. Who's going to clean this up? And drive across town to get more? That's twelve dollars wasted!

When the energy cools down, I sigh with relief and throw my defective pepper spray on to the counter.

"Girl! What the hell are you doing here?"

"Babe, I never left! I'm in unemployed-mode, remember? I specifically asked you if it was cool if I went into unemployed-mode at your apartment."

"I didn't know that meant you were staying a second night! I didn't know what you meant at all! Who would know what that means?"

Kierra hugs me. "Shhh, babe, it's okay. I'm here."

This is her move when someone's mad at her and she doesn't understand why, which is frequent enough for her to have a move for. Usually I roll my eyes at it, but I must need a hug because I start to tear up.

The cathartic moment is ruined by a loud banging on my door. Someone's trying to get in. Who the hell is it now? I look at Kierra, she's just as scared as I am. We hear a door open in the apartment next to mine, and a woman says, "What do you want?" as clear as if she was in the room with us.

So, it wasn't my apartment door someone was banging on, it was my neighbor's. It must be the weed or I just didn't realize how thin these walls are.

"I want to TALK to you, Jane," an angry man says in the hall, his voice raised.

"Well I don't want to TALK to YOU! Leave me alone!" The neighbor slams her door shut and locks the knob, deadbolt, and chain.

The man bangs on her door again, and he yells. "JANE, I JUST WANT TO TALK. WE NEED TO TALK."

He knocks and knocks, his knuckles must be bloody, and repeats her name in different intonations. JANE. JANE. JANE. The neighbor starts blaring Death Metal music at full volume to drown out the sound of his yelling. JANE. JANE. JANE. JANE...

The frantic, distorted guitar riffs make my brain feel like it's going to explode. JANE. JANE. JANE. JANE. JANE. JANE. JANE. JANE. JANE. JANE. JANE. JANE. JANE. JANE. JANE. JANE. JANE. JANE. COME ON, JANE. It's gone on too long, when will it end? This chaos is overwhelming! JANE. JANE. JANE. JANE. JANE. JANE. I'm going to lose my mind... JANE. JANE. JANE. JANE. JANE. JANE. JANE. JANE. JANE. JANE. JANE. JANE. JANE. I JUST WANT TO TALK, JANE. JANE. JANE. JANE. JANE. JANE. JANE. JANE. JANE. JANE. JANE. JAN...

"Kierra, this is freaking me out."

...NE. JANE. JANE. JANE. JANE. JANE. JANE. JANE. JANE. JANE. JANE. JANE. JANE. JANE.

JANE. JANE. JANE. JANE. JANE. JANE. JANE. JANE...
"At least we know your neighbor's name now."
...E. JANE. JANE. JANE. JA...
"Yeah, I'm not forgetting it anytime soon."
...ANE. JANE. JANE. JANE. JANE. JANE. JANE. JANE. JANE. JANE. JANE. JANE. WE NEED TO TALK JANE. JANE. JANE. JANE. JANE. JANE. JANE. JANE. JANE...
"Like Jane Doe."
...JANE. JANE. JANE. JANE. JANE...
"What?"
...JANE. JANE. JANE...
"Her name, it's like Jane Doe."
...JANE. JANE. JANE. JANE. JANE. JANE...
"That's not funny, Kierra."
...JANE. JANE. JANE...
"What do you mean funny? I don't get it."
...JANE. JANE JANE. LET ME IN, JANE. LET ME IN. LET ME IN.

I really wish I hadn't smoked that weed.

CHAPTER 3

I wake up with a pounding headache, the name "Jane" still echoing in my brain. JANE. JANE. JANE.

I did NOT get my beauty sleep and with the 9am yard work going on outside I don't see any point in trying. I'm not like Kierra who's snoring like a hog in my living room (that's not helping either) and can sleep through almost everything.

I need coffee, and the fridge is empty, so I'll check out the cute cafe down the block. After my face is on, I put together an outfit, settling on a pair of black jeans with a black cropped tee that features a portrait of Janis Joplin singing. Black heels too—I love an all black ensemble, It speaks to me. Looking good despite how I feel, I stumble out the door and lock it behind me.

Ryan, the manager, is leaving the apartment next to mine (apartment 201, not Jane's) and locking the door while I do the same. We exchange an awkward glance and he smiles.

My face gets hot, and I avert eye contact just a little. "Is that one going up for rent too? Or are you still renovating it?"

He looks confused and frowns. "No, I live here. You know that."

"You live next-door?"

"Yeah, I told you when I was showing you the laundry room. One of the benefits of this complex is that I live onsite, and I can respond to maintenance requests quickly. And I said that I live next-door in two-oh-one, because I'm still renovating the first-floor units. You don't remember that?"

All I remember about the laundry room is that it's in a spooky basement that felt haunted. I know it's just some machines and probably a storage area, but it gave me the creeps. Maybe he did say something and I just missed it while I was getting ghost-vibes. "I guess I didn't hear you."

Ryan smiles. "I hope it's not too big of a disappointment."

"No, it's fine. Were you able to sleep with the noise last night?"

"What noise?"

That's weird. I almost tell him about Jane, but I

don't want to get her in trouble. And how could he not have heard that? "There was literally a man yelling."

"Huh. Maybe I was already knocked out. I'm a super deep sleeper."

How could anyone sleep through that? Even Kierra couldn't. I'm too groggy and coffee is calling—no point in trying to figure this out. I thank him (for what I don't know) and wish him a nice day.

The cafe is a ghost town, it's unnerving. And from the taste of this cold brew, I can guess why. It's totally bitter and overpriced, but I need the caffeine, so I load it up with cream and sugar to make it bearable. When I step out of the cafe there's some guy hanging out on the street. Dark skinned, kind of chunky, but kind of cute. He looks me up and down, then kisses at me in an embarrassing, obvious kind of way. "Hey, you're beautiful. Gimme your name."

This dude is way too cheesy; I feel the chunks rising. I fake a smile and keep walking, hoping he'll leave me alone. He calls after me. "You gotta boyfriend? You're a real woman, right?"

Idiots. Sometimes, I just CAN'T with men. So simple, no depth. I'm just glad he didn't follow me. I'm almost back to the apartment, and there's Jane again, walking in front of me to our building. I still can't see her face, but she's holding a cup of coffee too. I call to her, raising my voice and waving my hand. "Hey girl! I'm your new neighbor...?"

She does it again! She speeds up and closes the door behind her, this time with a loud slam that hurts my head. And she definitely heard me this time; she's ignoring me. I just wanted to introduce myself and ask where I can get decent coffee. What a bitch. Or maybe she has some sort of social anxiety; our generation is all fucked up.

Or maybe she's just embarrassed about last night. I guess I would be too. She's not the first girl to fall for a man who turned out to be a psycho, loser, or freak.

I return to my apartment and, in my caffeinated state, the sun coming through the window looks inviting instead of blinding. Kierra is awake, scrunched up on the couch and scrolling through social media on her phone. Her voice is lazy and she doesn't look up. "Hey, babe."

"Hey, girl. I ran into the apartment manager this morning. Apparently, he lives next-door, but I don't remember him telling me. Is that weird?"

She perks up a little without taking her eyes away from the screen. "Oh yeah, Ryan! I talked to him yesterday when you were out. Really nice guy. Real hot too, right?"

"You talked with him yesterday?"

"Yeah, I saw him in the hall. He said that maybe he knew me, he recognized my voice, but I don't think I've met him…but he does have this vibe of someone you've met before. You know what I mean?"

Recognized her voice? Like from their phone conversation when she was posing as my ex-housemate/landlord? "Yeah, I guess so. So, you don't think it's weird that he lives next-door? There's nothing off about him?"

"Nah, he seems like a really nice guy."

"He said he didn't hear anything last night—he's a heavy sleeper. How could anyone sleep through all that noise?"

"I had a boyfriend like that once; he had three super loud alarms, and you could slap him across the face and he'd still oversleep. I thought he was dead once, it freaked me out." She goes back into her phone, switching to a video app and scrolling through the feed with the sound at full blast.

"Kierra?"

Kierra looks at me with glazed eyes while a high pitched sped-up version of a pop song plays from her phone. "Yeah?"

"Unless you're helping me unpack, I need some time to myself before practice tonight."

"Babe, I can't, I'm in unemployed-mode."

"Goodbye, Kierra."

―

I bang on the wall to Jane's apartment, hoping she'll get the hint that she's being way too loud. Max and Kierra have already given up on practice and are on their phones. I can't let Jane ruin our first official practice at my new place. We have to be able to play here. Maybe this apartment has been empty for a while and she just isn't used to having a next-door neighbor. I thought blasting death metal was bad, but this drone music she has on is even worse. And there's these weird yells and screams and pig squeals. Is she doing a sex thing? Or…do people have pet pigs? Is that even allowed here?

The sounds continue so I bang again. And she turns the music up! What the hell? She IS a bitch.

"Did she really just do that?" Max says as they join me at the wall.

"What a bitch. I tried to be nice to her, you know."

We both bang on the wall even harder and start yelling. "You're too loud!"

She turns the music up, blowing out her speakers and further distorting the chopped-and-screwed accordion hell. Kierra joins us, we keep pounding with the combined power of our fists. "Shut the fuck up!"

I see a puff of plaster-powder in the corner of my eye. We're damaging the wall! "Wait!"

We stop our assault and look down to see a thick crack at chest-level. I've been here less than three days, and I've already damaged my apartment.

I bend down to inspect the damage and notice there's something reflective inside the crack. More chunks fall off as I prod the crack lightly, there was a hole here already that was poorly patched. And there's light leaking out of it. Is that a lens? Is this what I think it is?

I put my eye to the hole. It's what I thought: a peephole. The fisheye lens gives me a full view of Jane's living room and kitchen. And the scene is wild.

Jane is in a worker's jumpsuit, but it's clear plastic and she's wearing nothing but bikini bottoms underneath, holding a medieval-looking whip with metal chains on the end. The living room is mostly clear of furniture, and there's a naked man on all fours wearing a way too realistic dead-pig mask. He's covered in bloody marks. Jane struts around him, in a menacing way, and I can finally get a look at her. She's clocky (in a hot way) and I'm 99.99% sure she's trans too. Oh, the bulge in her panties—she's definitely trans. I'm not judging that she's doing sex work, a lot of us girls have to, but why does it have to be so loud? Where's the respect?

Max nudges me aside, turning their cap backwards to look. "Is that a peephole? Are you kidding me? Let me see."

"I wanna see too!" Kierra says.

I shush them, still reeling from the discovery that someone installed this peephole in my apartment. Does it go both ways? Who put it in? "I don't think we should be looking; it feels wrong. I should just tell Ryan to fix it."

"Oh my god. It's a BDSM scene."

Kierra shoves Max out of the way. "What the eff? She's got a pigman in there! Is that legal?"

I push Kierra aside to look. Jane is strangling the pigman now and force feeding him bacon while he's being all dramatic about it and acting like he hates it. I don't kink-shame, but as a vegan, and an animal lover, this was making me sick to my stomach. "Oh my god."

Jane grabs something that looks like giant pliers with teeth on each end. It's plugged in. It's one of those tools slaughterhouses use to stun pigs. I recognize it from some anti-animal-cruelty videos I've seen. Is she going to use that on him? Couldn't that kill him?

She clamps the man's neck with the stunner. Burn marks and smoke begin to appear across his neck as he shakes, and his body collapses. He's not moving. What the fuck just happened. This can't be real. He can't be dead. But he's not moving. He's still not moving.

CHAPTER 4

After running errands all day to prepare for our show at The Hi Hat next week, I'm finally back to my building. Thank god too, I'm exhausted.

This place still gives me the creeps a little at night. I guess I'm not used to living here, or maybe I'm just traumatized by my neighbor. The scene last night was gruesome, and I'm trying to keep it out of my head today—but it keeps popping in. What did I see? I know it was most likely roleplay, but that man's death seemed so real. And he lay on the floor until I gave up and went to bed. The man—or the body—was gone by the time I woke up. I feel sick, and I can't stop asking myself: what if it was a session with a client that went wrong and she actually killed the guy?

My shoulder aches from the weight of my *Wizard of Oz* themed Moschino PVC tote bag full of flyers. I picked them up from the print shop earlier that day. Max designed the flyer for the show, and it looks amazing. At first I was a little shy about having my face featured so prominently on it (the graphic was stylized but it was still unmistakably me), but Max and Kierra hyped me up about it and made me feel like a celeb. I'm the lead singer-songwriter of Totally Toxic, after all.

I spent hours today giving people flyers with my face on them and posting them throughout downtown, but there's still a ton left. I'm beyond exhausted from lugging them around. It's time to drop everything and relax—but I'll put one more up in the lobby of the apartment by the mailboxes before I go up the stairs.

It better be a quiet night; beauty sleep is overdue.

I freeze. Is that a face? Is someone in the elevator? No, it's just reflection and shadow. Something's different about the elevator, and it looked like there was a face in that little square window for a second. Is the folding gate open? Is that what changed? Maybe they repaired it—but the out-of-order sign is still on the door. I wish it was working, even one flight of stairs feels like a lot right now.

As I reach the top of the stairs the light in the hallway flickers on and off, plunging half of my path into darkness. The light reappears for a moment—and then darkness again. My breath quickens, but I still walk toward the eerie void that surrounds my apartment door. I should tell Ryan about this busted light. It's so dark, and my heart is pounding in my head. Did the bulb just die?

I'm almost to my door when the space is illuminated again with a crackling buzz, revealing a tall, spidery man before me. He's standing in front of the apartment across from mine, staring at me. I scream and jump back and tighten my grip on my tote. Where the hell did he come from? I reach for my pepper spray, but it's not there. I forgot to replace it!

He just stands there, staring, holding something in a plastic shopping bag. His face is blank, but I think he's blushing and he sniffs like a kid with a stuffy nose. Is this who lives in the apartment across from me? This guy is spooky, he's so tall but he's thinner than a potato chip. He'd look out of place anywhere. A wrinkled green button up, messy hair, white and pale, and he's young—early 20s I'd guess.

I laugh nervously. "Hi…you scared me. I'm Lenora, your new neighbor." I don't offer my hand.

He looks like he wants to say something, but he just gawks at me and sniffs and swallows. I rarely get the feeling of wanting to cover up, but I just want his eyes off of me. He's not blocking my door—I should just leave. That's enough of this incel.

"Nice to meet you!" I say as I unlock my door as fast as I can and slam it behind me. I drop my tote and keys on the console table by the entrance and settle into the couch, letting out a big exhale. Is this apartment complex full of creeps?

My laptop is open next to me and it dings to get my attention. It's Max, they've sent a message to the Totally Toxic group chat: "I was right, it's a cam show. She's got tons of videos like these on her profile."

Their next message is a link, and I click on it, taking me to BeautifullyBroken69's profile on LonelyCams. It's Jane for sure. She's not live now, but there are a ton of videos and she has a small following. There must be a camera set up. How did I miss that last night?

I get up and look through the peephole to try to find the camera. It's a little camouflaged with the dark-colored wall, but it's there at the back of the room, and there's a laptop on a chair next to it. No sign of Jane; she must not be home. I guess I was too focused on the slaughterhouse scene and floor-corpse to notice the camera before. I reply to Max: "I see the camera. How did you find this?"

"I just searched for 'trans dom force feeds pigman bacon pvc' on a few cam sites until I found her profile."

"He's not dead?"

"Nah. He 'dies' in other videos too, some of these have some pretty impressive special FX."

Kierra chimes in: "WHOA."

I scroll through more of her videos. They have titles like "Extreme BDSM swing torture party girldick," "Circus clussy hits different t girl clown porn xxx," "Necro incest fantasy dead daddy roleplay," "Probed by two tranny alien babes," "Human doll hypno gang-bang trans puppet girl sucks 4 giant cocks," "T-girl masked psycho eats dick for dinner," "Focus group force fem fantasy office roleplay."

There's a cast of about three guys, the pigman, a guy with a cliche "mom" heart tattoo on his arm who wears a baby mask, and a buff, well-endowed guy with a wolf mask. There's also another trans woman in a few of the videos, a tall tan Asian woman who wears her long black hair up in a tight ponytail. She's absolutely gorgeous, like a model.

I make the mistake of reading the comments on some of her videos.

wtf did I just watch

I'm straight but I want her cock am I gay?

Hideous and distorted bodies! Sickening abomination

Shemales are such perfect goddesses <3

It's 3am and I have work tomorrow I've never had a girlfriend and I don't have any friends and I'm jerking off to two "women" because I want them to fuck me. I need to get my life together, I hit a new low

Her dick is bigger than mine

Wow he has amazing tits for a man, trans so beautiful. I'm bisexual

Why isn't this on a gay site? Disturbing!

"Fucking a tranny is like a threesome" that's what I always say

If a real tranny impregnated a biological woman I bet the baby would be beautiful

I'm fingering myself with coke in my nose, i want to get fuked by a trans

where can I find shemales near me? please

Are these the people living amongst us? It's completely cringe.

We share our findings with each other in the group chat, poring over Jane's life's work. It seems wrong but strangely addicting, and I almost feel like I have the right to know. She's been involving me in all this with how loud she's being. She ruined our band practice!

CHAPTER 5

I swear those flyers were still in my tote bag by the door, but they aren't here. I don't remember taking them out. Sometimes I get the creepy feeling that someone's been in my apartment and moved things around when I'm away, but then I remember that's actually true—and it's Kierra. I text her about it (who knows what she does when I'm away), but she said she's never touched them. Maybe I did move them, this heatwave is completely cooking my brain. Is it this hot every year? Or is this whole damn planet getting fried by climate change? And there's this weird chemical smell throughout the building—I'll mention it to Ryan when he comes, he's supposed to be on his way to fix my air conditioner.

    Of course my AC gives out as soon as I really need

it. This room is boiling, and I swear I'm going to faint before Ryan arrives. There's a knock at the door and it's him, like he could read my mind. To his credit, he's a good manager. He fixed the flickering light before I could say anything, I always see him sweeping the halls, and now he's responding to a maintenance request within 30 minutes. Maybe it really is good to have a manager on site, as long as he's cool.

I let Ryan in, he's wearing a tight white shirt and black jeans with a navy handkerchief in his back pocket and holding his toolkit. There's something so sexy about a man who can fix things. His smile is warm and inviting, as usual. "Unit on the fritz?"

"Yeah, I don't know what happened."

"Let's take a look." Ryan gets down on his knees and pulls out his screwdriver in a fluid motion. He has the panel off so fast, and he's in the machine before I could even take another breath. He furrows his brow and squints. "Yea, it's totally busted. We're going to have to get you a new one."

I can't get through this heat wave without AC. My brain will be so fried—I won't be able to write songs. The last time this happened at my other place it took weeks for the landlord to replace it. "Great. How long until I get a new one?"

Ryan stands up and wipes off his forehead with his

handkerchief and sighs in a way that tells me he has more bad news. "Yea, normally I need to go through the company and submit a request, they get it from their vendor and it can take a few days…"

"Fuck."

"But, y'know what? I'll just pick up a unit from Home Depot right now. I can say it was an emergency and convince them to reimburse me."

My panic subsides a little. "For real? You'd do that?"

"Yea, you need AC. Hang tight, I'll be right back."

He leaves before I can even thank him, and he's back before I can even sit down. Ryan installs the new air conditioning unit like it's nothing and turns it on. A triumphant breeze fills the room. It works even better than my previous one, and I feel a massive sense of relief wash over my body with the cool air.

The feverish feeling of the heatwave invading my apartment and the panic of not having working AC disappears.

He wipes the sweat off his forehead. "Is there anything else I can do for you while I'm here?"

My eyes dart toward the cracked wall and peephole for a millisecond, it's covered by a picture of my mom's dog Snowball. "No, I'm good. Thanks again."

"Alright, I'll be seeing you."

I almost forget about the weird smell. "Oh, here's something: there's this strong smell in the hall sometimes, like chemicals or something."

"It's paint thinner, part of the renovations. Sorry about that, I'll make sure the guys set up better ventilation. Is that all? Anything else?"

I can't think of anything so Ryan leaves with a smile and a nod and I collapse on my couch. Damn, he didn't have to do that. He really knows what he's doing and takes his job seriously; he's definitely the best apartment manager I've ever had. I sigh, letting out all of my tensions and enjoy the softness of my couch, the feeling of my bare feet on the soft shag carpet, and the cool air flowing across my body. I close my eyes.

I jump when loud music is abruptly turned on next-door. It's dark. What time is it? I must have fallen asleep. And what is this music? It sounds like EDM with electronic bells and anime girls talking and giggling over the track. It's so loud.

My phone buzzes next to me and the light of the screen burns my eyes. I check the time, and it's almost midnight and there's a million notifications on my phone. The most recent is a message from Max in the Totally Toxic group chat that says "LENORA!"

I open the group chat, Max and Kierra have been trying to get my attention. I scroll up to earlier in the day.

Today 3:52 PM
Me: I have AC again!!
Max: Nice
Kierra: i'm bored.

Today 11:01 PM
Kierra: are you guys up?
        omg you guys go to Jane's livestream
        it's.
        so.
        goofy.
Max: You've been watching it?
Kierra: yeah I was bored
Max: Whoa
        Is that peanut butter and jelly?
Kierra: i think so!!!!
Max: Is that the pigman from before?
        How does she get the jars to float like that
Kierra: i think it's the same guy?!?
        strings?!?!!
Max: I don't think so
        They're moving too much
        I bet it's a guy in one of those bright green bodysuits
Kierra: like a green screen? so she has two guys in

	there?
	lenora can you look through the hole?
	to see if there's a green suit man?!!?!
Max:	It has to be
	Lenora?
Kierra:	babe.
	lenora!!!
Max:	LENORA!

I'm groggy and I'm having trouble comprehending what they're talking about but I check in anyway.

Me:	Fell asleep on the couch. Let me see

I fumble around in the dark, using the screen of my phone as a flashlight. The photo of Snowball that's covering the peephole is vibrating with the bass of the loud music. And as I bring my eye to the tiny hidden window the thought that I shouldn't be doing this pops into my head and it cuts through my nap fog. But I'm already looking. And it's not like I haven't seen her videos before. This is just another angle to what she's already broadcasting publicly.

Jane is wearing a red bikini and a large, floppy, wizard hat, and she's waving a wand. Next to her is a man in one of those green screen suits they have for the movies, holding open jars of peanut butter and jelly, lifting them up and down to make it look like they're floating. Behind the green suit man (in front of the camera) is a naked guy on his hands and knees. It's hard to see him but he's covered in peanut butter and jelly and has slices of white bread stuck to his body. So, she's supposed to be some sort of sexy sandwich wizard?

Me:	Yeah, there's a green suit guy
	Holding the jars
Max:	I knew it!
Kierra:	thanks lenora!!
Me:	It's so loud
	I need sleep
Max:	Maybe you can complain to the manager?
Me:	I don't want to get her in trouble, this is probably her bread and butter
	Literally
Kierra:	LMAO
Me:	Maybe I can talk to her
	Tomorrow
Max:	Yea
Me:	If she'll finally talk to me
	She kind of seems like a bitch
	Ugh.

I grab my laptop and click the link from Kierra to watch Jane's show from the official angle. The man covered in peanut butter and jelly sandwiches is wearing mime makeup. The sandwiches are piling up on the tarp, and the jars of peanut butter and jelly really do seem like they're floating. Is this supposed to be sexy? Or is this some sort of performance art thing?

The views on this stream are low, fewer than twenty, and it doesn't seem like any of them are giving her tips. Is she making any money doing this? Is she just really desperate and trying out all sorts of weird scenes to see what sticks? Is this her only income? What's your deal, Jane?

CHAPTER 6

"You're going with Ryan? You mean like my apartment manager, Ryan?"

Kierra looks at herself in my full-length mirror to make sure her hiking outfit is fitting right and serving the perfect combination of athletic and 90's grunge. "Yea, he told me about this hiking spot, and I said we should go sometime. Wanna come with us?"

How often has Kierra been talking to Ryan? She practically lives here lately (sharing her mom's old house with her drug addicted brother Michael is too depressing, so I gave her an extra key), but I can't imagine they've had that much time together. Suddenly they're close enough to make plans with each other. How close are they? "Wait, is this a date?"

She wraps a finger around a lock of her hair and checks her makeup. "You know, I hadn't really thought about it. I think it's just a friend-thing."

I mentally flick away the tiny speck of jealousy in my chest. "But you like him."

"I mean, he's hot, and nice, but I barely know him. You should come, it'll be fun! You like hiking, right? We're going to Cobb Estate; there's ruins from an old hotel or something at the top of the mountain."

I'm in a songwriting rut, and I want to believe that finally having some time to myself will help me out of it. But if I'm being honest, I don't think it's Kierra that's the problem. If anything, it's my fucked up sleep schedule thanks to Jane. I really need to do something about that.

Maybe getting some fresh air and exercise would be good for my mood and creativity. Hunching over my notebook and keyboard is starting to take its toll. Plus, I wouldn't mind seeing Ryan's fit body in motion—just to look. "Alright, I'll go. I need a few minutes to get ready."

"Rad!"

"And he's gonna be cool with it? He doesn't think it's a date, right?"

"Who knows what guys think. It'll be fine. And if he's weird about it, he sucks."

I put on my face and a hiking outfit: an American Apparel onesie I've had for years, shorts, and chunky platform sneakers.

"I'm ready!" I announce and twirl for my adoring audience: Kierra. She bounces on the couch and claps before hopping to her feet.

We head over to knock on Ryan's door. He answers wearing a vintage Garfield t-shirt, Nikes, short red 80s-style gym shorts, and an outdoorsy backpack. God, he's easy on the eyes, and he definitely doesn't skip leg day.

"Hi, Kierra, Hi, Lenora! You coming too?" he says with a crooked smile.

I smile back. "Yeah, I need to move my body."

"Great! The more the merrier."

Kierra drives us through Pasadena and up to the foot of the mountain in her old Jeep Wrangler with the top down. My body relaxes as the air turns from smoggy to crisp with the gentle smell of oak and eucalyptus. It's warm, but the heatwave broke over the weekend, and being outside in the barely 80-degree weather combined with the breeze feels cool in comparison.

We walk through the old gates and into the park where we're greeted by a large clearing with a number of winding trails and towering eucalyptus trees. The tall grass is brown from the dry air, but the leaves on the trees show off their green, and bird songs surround us.

The city is just outside, but here we are transported. This place belongs to nature, it feels wild yet peaceful, but at the same time, it feels like ours. It's gorgeous. Just the inspiration I need.

"Wow!" Kierra says, spinning around with her hands up. "I can't believe I've never been here."

Ryan takes a deep breath savoring the clean air, holding the straps of his backpack. "Isn't it great? And on weekdays, there aren't many people here."

I don't go into nature enough; this is just what I need. "We should bring Max here; they would love it."

We walk past the concrete foundations of buildings long gone, and now covered in colorful graffiti of stoner aliens, crude political statements, and one-line eulogies. I whisper one to myself, *rest in peace JuiceBoy666*, as we enter the tunnel of trees and begin our trek up the mountain.

It's not long before we get to our first lookout spot to take a quick break and check out the view. Ryan hands each of us a cold water bottle, and I wipe sweat off my brow as I take a refreshing sip. It feels good to sweat, to move my body (going to the gym used to be a regular thing for me, but I had to give up my membership—too expensive). And the view is incredible.

"Wooooooooooow," Kierra says, before stretching out like a starfish, doing a power pose to soak in the panoramic beauty. There are more trees leading up to the park than I realized, and it creates a sea of green before giving way to the urban area. Tiny cars peacefully travel down the highways, like a perfect model city. Under the blue clouded expanse of the sky, you can even see downtown, a little hazy island that you'd never know was full of activity from here.

Ryan turns to me with his signature smile and a warm gaze. "I've been here a dozen times, and I'll never get tired of this view."

I almost whisper, "It's gorgeous."

We continue up the trail until we reach the top of the mountain to find more ruins, discarded parts from an old mountain railway, and even some plaques explaining the history of the place. We each take turns screaming into the echo phone, a mounted metal cone that projects your voice to what feels like all of LA.

"Follow Totally Toxic on Instagram, at kierra underscore toxxxic with three Xs!" Kierra yells. "Underscore the symbol, not the word!"

"I'm the king of the world!" Ryan goes, with a little shyness, before he turns to us for approval of his dated reference.

I want to say, "trans liberation now," but I don't want to out myself, so instead I shout the more generic: "Freedom for the people!"

The hike is longer than I expected, but I don't even care, I feel alive and invigorated. I just climbed a mountain; I can do anything. Coming down the trail feels easy, and the sun is starting to set as we descend, displaying pink and gold in the sky.

I hear Ryan let out a soft gasp. He digs his feet into the dirt and puts his arms out, and Kierra, and I bump into them, sliding slightly on the loose ground with the sudden stop. He whispers. "Don't move." And then I see it.

Crouched in the bushes next to the trail is a mountain lion or some other big wildcat. It's less than 10 feet away from us. I feel a bolt of concentrated fear rush through my body and activate my adrenal glands. I want to run, but I know that would be the worst thing I could do. I feel Kierra jerk away, but Ryan quickly grasps his arm around hers without turning or breaking his protective stance. He has her secured, stopping her from acting on her potentially life-ending instinct. His tone is hushed but steady. "Don't run, it'll think you're prey. Stay behind me."

I don't know what a mountain lion looks like when it's hangry, but I'm pretty sure I'm seeing it now. Kierra's sudden movement seems to have changed its attitude toward us. My heart pounds and I swallow as my hands grip Ryan's outstretched arm. He slowly bends down and picks up a rock and then raises his hands up, arms wide, making himself as big as possible. His voice is deep and booming, and I can feel it vibrating from his rib cage. "HEY! HEY! GET OUT OF HERE. GO! SCAT!"

He throws the rock, landing his shot just close enough to the beast that it gets spooked, and his impressive presence causes the big cat to run off. Once it's far enough away we catch our breath. Kierra moans. "Ugh! I literally just died right there."

I put my hand on my chest to steady my rapid heartbeat. I can't stop shaking. It was so close. "Like what the actual fuck."

Ryan nods his head slightly. "We're okay now."

I hug him out of instinct, he's steady and strong and I want to stop shaking and I want to catch my breath. He wraps his arms around me, and Kierra immediately makes it a group hug. She pushes me closer to him and I'm struck by his smell. His musk is intoxicating, and I feel my body relax and at the same time a fire deep between my legs lights. Shit.

—

I'm lying in bed in my PJs, fresh from the post-hike shower, and I'm horny. So hot and bothered that even the orgasmic moans of The Jane Show next-door are appealing and sort of turning me on. It's crazy how loud it is, that I can hear it all the way from my bedroom. I don't know how Ryan sleeps through this. I wonder if his room is on the other side of this wall. I wonder if he's lying in bed too.

In my mind, I replay him saving us and remember his scent and warmth. I slide a hand down to my crotch and lightly stroke over it, teasing myself.

My bedroom door cracks open and light spills into the room. I bolt up to see Kierra's face peeking out, her big eyes even wider than usual. "Psst, Lenora!"

The mood is so killed. "What!"

She holds her phone up, Jane's stream is playing on it, but it's too small for me to see what's going on. "You gotta see this."

"I'm trying to sleep. I'm not in the mood to see Jane jack off a human pizza or whatever weird sex thing she's cooked up this time."

"No, you don't understand, this is another level." She almost sounds shaken.

Of course I have to know what's happening now. If something crazy is happening next-door, I should at least know about it. I follow Kierra to the peephole and take a breath as I put my eye up to it.

Jane is wearing a leather harness and a vaguely fascist military commander cap. She has a man strapped to a plastic-covered dining table with tight, thick leather straps across his body. Her friend, the other trans woman that's appeared in some of her videos, is also there. She's wearing a matching harness and uniform but doesn't have the same cap—you can't cover that perfect high pony.

The man is bleeding, and his face is red. Jane smashes her junk into his mouth as she runs a straight razor up his back. Her friend laughs and cracks a leather strap against her palm. The man's skin splits and blood flows out in pools, redder than ever on a pale body that must never see the sun. He's covered with cuts, and it's hard to tell from here, but I think he has rows of needles in his back too.

Jane grabs his hair and pushes his face into her, forcing him to take her in his mouth deeper. Her friend is stroking herself, getting hard and ready to enter him. He whimpers as he sucks Jane's length, and she licks his blood off the straight razor with a wicked smile. I feel my stomach lurch. I don't like blood. I don't like this.

Maybe I'm less kinky than I thought, because that's more than enough for me. For good. I pull away from the peephole and turn to Kierra who's watching from her phone, hypnotized by the scene. She jumps when I place my hand on her shoulder. "Kierra, what the fuck is this?"

"I don't know! She's your neighbor!"

"God. I think I've had enough of The Jane Show. Can we just pretend this isn't happening?"

"But do you think that's legal? Should we do something?"

"She's not doing anything wrong, I'm sure these guys are loving it. There are plenty of perverts watching that would love to switch places with that guy. It's just beyond kinky and really, really not my thing."

"I'm texting Max."

"Whatever, just don't bother me with this again. No more Jane Show. From now on, she's just a noisy neighbor."

Kierra makes an exaggerated puppy-dog begging face, pouting out her bottom lip. "Really?"

"I'm going to bed."

I lie in bed and sigh, staring up at the ceiling, willing my body to relax and my eyelids to get heavy. I can still hear the faint moans next-door. They've taken on a sinister quality. My mind jumps to the mountain lion and then the blood and then the hug. Why can't this be normal? I just wanted a relatively peaceful, private, and comfortable home where I could write songs in peace. Jane is ruining everything.

I need to talk to her somehow. Do I have to wait outside her door until she comes out just to have a conversation? Jane, what's wrong with you? Why won't you talk to me?

CHAPTER 7

After a short drive to Highland Park in Max's van, we set up our gear on the small black stage in the back of The Hi Hat. We're the opening act, so we're early, and it's completely empty inside. I hope people show up. The brick wall doesn't look great as a background; I wish we had a banner to hang behind us. It'll look better when the stage lights are on though, maybe even give off a 90s music video vibe.

It's our first show in almost two months and the debut of our new song, *Fraud Bitches*. I'd hoped to have at least three new songs to play, but Jane's craziness got in the way of that. We haven't even practiced as much as I'd like.

Kierra's finishing up my makeup in the rundown

backstage area—she always does my makeup for shows. She never fails to make me look no less than amazing, and knowing that helps with the pre-show jitters. She attempts to open up a box of false lashes, but I brush her hand away. "Kierra I don't want lashes—"

"You're never any fun!" she says and stomps her foot like a two-year-old.

"I don't need anything impairing my vision on stage, girl."

Max is ready to go, as usual. They're always fully prepared before they even pick us up. Their ball cap is missing and their short blonde hair is pulled back in a little enby-bun. Distressed jeans, a black sports bra that says "BOY" on the band, Freddy Mercury makeup, and a leather jacket—our bassist looks pretty fucking hot.

Kierra and I are wearing matching black, pleather miniskirts and platform pleaser boots with hot pink tank tops. We have our hair in matching high ponies, too. My hair is very thick and wavy, and even though I love it, I'm not sure I want it in my face all night long. Plus the high ponies make us look super femmed-up.

"I love the way pink looks on your complexion, Lenora!" Kierra says as she applies the blush.

"Thanks, babe," I reply, blushing for real. The pink looks just as hot on Kierra, but she could pull off anything, really.

Our confidence is turned up to eleven when we walk out onto the stage, ready to put on a good show, until butterflies fill my chest after seeing the audience—the venue is packed, shoulder-to-shoulder. I thought we'd be performing for a small crowd (we're the opening act after all), not so many people. They're cheering as we walk out on stage. I look at Max and Kierra and they share my elated expression. It turns out Kierra's social media magic really works! Those followers are real people, and a ton of them showed up for us! And all those flyers I put up around town, they must have paid off too. I let out a WOOO. "Let's go, bitches!"

Kierra gets comfortable behind her drums, Max picks up their bass and gives it a kiss on the neck, and I strut over to my keyboard and mic. "We're Totally Toxic! Are you ready for us?"

The crowd goes wild, jumping and screaming and raising their phones and drinks. Kierra taps out the beat with her drumsticks and we launch into our most popular song, *These Lips Could Kill*. The PA system sends our energetic and melodic vibrations into the crowd.

This crowd is incredible, they know our music and they're rocking out! Max goes insane on the bass, and Kierra whips her ponytail around as she furiously knocks out the beat. Blue and pink stage lights move across our bodies. The girls in the front dance wildly and scream the lyrics along with me as loud as they can. "Lipstick toxic, poison kiss! Take a bite outta you, take this!"

We finish with our latest song *Fraud Bitches* and the fans absolutely lose it, there's even a crowd surfer wearing checkered vans like he's out of a 90s pop-punk music video. Perfect.

Our set ends, and we squeal, and high-five each other backstage. We emerge and wade into the sea of people, following Kierra to the bar after getting hugs from friends who showed. It's like we're celebrities, fans are congratulating us and buying us drinks. Maybe a few too many drinks—definitely more than I'm used to. Down the bar I see a familiar face. It's Ryan! He gives a casual smile and wave. Kierra sees him too and leans over me, making dramatic gestures for him to come over. "Have a driiiiiink with uuuussss!"

Ryan grins and joins us. He puts his face close to ours and yells so we can hear him over the loud music of the second act that just started. "Hey, girls! Hey, Max!"

I cup my hand over my mouth and lean into him. "What're you doing here? Isn't it past your bedtime?"

He chuckles and does the same, getting closer, and

his scent is intoxicating. "A little. I saw the flyer in the lobby! You were incredible!"

We all share one more drink. Max disappears with some curvy girl who's been chatting them up. Ryan, Kierra, and I find ourselves getting vegan tacos from the stand down the street to soak up the alcohol. York Ave is lined with string lights, trendy shops, street vendors, and food trucks serving cuisines from all over. The air is filled with the conversations of young couples, the laughter of friends, the clashing music of passing cars, and the rumble and smell of their engines. We sneak down a side street into a residential area to eat our delicious food, sitting together on a stone wall that lines the elevated lawn of someone's house.

I'm drunker than I thought and Ryan seems to be surrounded by some sort of halo that warms me up. I can't stop smiling. Kierra gets distracted by a churro cart and I feel a little dizzy, and I'm pulled toward Ryan by an invisible force. My head ends up on his shoulder.

"Lenora..." he says reluctantly, and turns his body a little away. I fall forward, not expecting him to move, and he catches me. We're embracing now, and I look up to his face; it's so close to mine. Does he know I'm trans? He looks a little shy, he's blushing and it's adorable. I give him a drunken smile and purse my lips. And then we're kissing—I don't know who started it but we're kissing—I grasp my arms around his strong body and he holds me tight and our lips and tongues dance. He's a really good kisser, and I feel tingling throughout my body and a flutter in my stomach. I shouldn't be doing this, I shouldn't be making out with this man—but it feels so good and I can't stop. His warm, gentle hands grasp my body, and I feel cherished for the first time in a long time.

CHAPTER 8

The rent check cashed and now my bank balance is a horror-show; it's becoming obvious that I underestimated how long I could make my savings last. But I also didn't anticipate my living situation to be so chaotic. We got a few hundred bucks from the show, and our three singles earned another few hundred that'll pay out some time this month, but all together that's not even barely-half of next month's rent. Max was right, we need new merch to sell. I have to bring in more money somehow. And maybe even cut down on my spending. Am I going to have to stop investing in my wardrobe? What a nightmare.

I close my laptop, and stuff my notebook and headphones into my bag and grab my keys. Before I leave, I check to make sure there aren't any surprises in the hallway using the peephole in my door. It's a new habit—I might be a little on edge. The hallway, distorted in the peephole lens, is empty, so I head out.

But when I'm in the hallway locking up, I realize I'm not alone. Strutting toward me like she's on a runway is a gorgeous and extremely tall woman with pleaser boots and a tight red dress. Her long black hair with the high ponytail makes it click for me—this is Jane's friend, the one who occasionally does scenes with her.

She smiles, blinding me with her perfect teeth, and gives me a little wave with her fingers as she passes by. I'm stunned for a moment by her otherworldly beauty and charisma. I wish I could look like that!

And like she was never here, she disappears up the stairwell that goes to the third floor. It's surreal seeing her in person after only having a view of her in videos and through the peephole. She's much more friendly than Jane, I wonder what her deal is. Where was she headed? Does she have other friends in the building? She couldn't live here, that would be too weird.

Back to reality, time to go to practice. There's a bus that will take me to the 7th Street Metro station but it's close enough to walk to, so that's what I usually do. Sometimes I wish I had a car (getting around LA without one is ridiculously slow), but taking transit is better—resist the car-culture. Then again what's the point, we're all going to burn anyway.

The practice space we rent two days a month is only a couple blocks from Chinatown station across the tracks. Max is excited about some sort of collaboration opportunity they won't say much about (kind of annoying), but I'm just looking forward to being able to focus on our music uninterrupted.

It might have been a risky move, but yesterday I slipped a note under Jane's door with my phone number on it. She already knows I want her to shut the fuck up. I figured if I could just meet with her, and we could get to know each other, we could be friendly. We're not going anywhere, we might as well make this as painless as possible. But she hasn't called or texted me yet. Maybe she never will.

"Hey!" a man in a plain black baseball cap and hoodie yells. He looks familiar. "Lenora! You're Lenora."

"Excuse me? How do you know my name?"

It's the guy from outside the coffee shop, and he's blocking the stairs to the subway entrance. He reaches into his hoodie and pulls out a folded up, dirty, and crinkled piece of paper, and opens it. It's the flyer for the show with my face on it. "This is you! Totally Toxic.

I looked you up."

I don't have social media, but I guess the band's accounts are getting popular. He's just walking around with a crumpled and stained picture of me? Totally gross, but I'd be lying if I said I wasn't a little flattered from being recognized. I try to get around him, but he moves to block me.

"What's your number? Give me your number."

"I'm in a hurry," I say and attempt to weave past him again, but he blocks my way.

He gets closer and hands me his phone. "C'mon. Let me get your number."

I give him a fake number and push past him into the station. Sometimes that's the only way guys leave you alone. *White Rabbit* by Jefferson Airplane plays in my headphones as I rush down the escalator. Chasing rabbits. Hopefully I'll get some space to think on the ride to Chinatown.

The practice space is one of many that are stuck together in what looks like a converted warehouse or private storage building. The floors are bare concrete, the walls are metal, and it's lit by less than flattering fluorescent lights. Walking down the halls you can hear every genre of music oozing out of each unit. Our space is one of the smaller ones and it's crammed with instruments from the five bands who share it—and the communal drum set that Kierra always complains about. It's not soundproof, but we can be as loud as we want and drown out our neighbors.

When I walk in, Max is sitting on the ratty maroon couch, watching something on their laptop. They're always early. Kierra hasn't arrived yet, but that's typical. If we don't come together, she always arrives last.

I sit down next to Max, it's some sort of music video, paused on a frame of a curvy white girl wearing a gold jumpsuit and sunray tiara. She's striking a pose over a green-screened star field.

"What's this?" I ask.

"Have you ever heard of Ghost Trick One?"

Nothing specific pops into my brain, but that doesn't mean I haven't heard of them. "Sounds vaguely familiar. Is this the collaboration you were talking about?"

They almost bite their nails but catch themself. "I'll tell you more when Kierra arrives."

I open my notebook to brainstorm song concepts, but I can't stop thinking about that kiss with Ryan. I was honestly shocked by how good a kisser he was, perfectly leading our dancing tongues without forcing it. I wonder if he's ever taken lessons—dancing lessons. The way his muscles flexed while he held me…so much strength but holding me so gently. I know it's a bad idea to date your apartment manager—I'm playing with fire—but I can't help it, I've fallen for him. And the alternatives are not impressing me.

Kierra finally stumbles in. She's wearing dark sunglasses and holding a nearly empty iced coffee. She's giving major "walk of shame" energy. Her voice is hoarse and uncharacteristically flat. "Babes. Hey."

I scoot closer to Max to make room for her on the couch. "Are you okay?"

"I'm fine. I had a fight with Michael last night about… I don't really want to talk about it." She collapses into the open space on the couch next to me and loudly slurps up the last drops of coffee through her straw.

"Kierra, have you ever heard of Ghost Trick One?"

She looks over her sunglasses at Max, revealing dark circles and bloodshot eyes. "The rapper girl you met at the show? The one you're trying to bang?"

Max blushes. "No—well, yeah. But that's unrelated. She wants to collaborate with us—and she's not really a rapper."

Kierra sighs, I haven't seen her this grumpy in awhile. "Max, she sucks. Her lyrics are stupid, and she has no rhythm."

Max pulls their laptop closer to themself, like

they're protecting the little Ghost Trick on the screen. "She's not a rapper, she doesn't need to be perfectly on-beat."

"Well, she can't sing, so…" Kierra waves her hands in circles, as if she's trying to conjure what Ghost Trick One is supposed to be.

I touch her on the arm to let her know to cool down. But Max is already pissed off and all tensed up. "Look, she said if we do a track with her she'll give us studio time. Like enough studio time to finish our album."

Kierra pushes her glasses up her face and slurps at the melted ice at the bottom of her cup in response.

Finish our album? I feel an electric flutter inside; this is exactly what we need. This could be huge. "She can get us into a studio?"

"Yeah, she's got a home studio, her parents are rich. And she's really not that bad of a…she's got potential. I think we can work with her."

Kierra snorts. "Yeah, if we want to ruin our reputation."

"Is anyone else offering us free studio time? Are there producers knocking down your door begging to work with us that you're hiding? We need this. Lenora, back me up on this."

"I mean…how bad could she be? Let's see the video."

Max turns their laptop to us. "Okay. Now, keep an open mind. Notice the sound and video production quality."

They hit play and psychedelic droning rises out of the laptop along with a steady 808 drum hit.

Spaced out into the universe, caked up in this universe
Aliens out of time in space flying, can't touch my verse
I'm the queen of Planet Sex from the 8th dimension
I'm on your radio, internet, your television's vision
Heat on fire, flames up, you know you wanna fuck me
Astral projection wrecking you, coming outta this sick-ass pussy

"Umm..operator? We have an emergency situation on Planet Sex. The aliens are attacking! Oh no, they're here to steal our pussies! Someone help us…"

SOS, EMERGENCY ON PLANET SEX! PLANET SEX, PLANET SEX! SOS ON PLANET SEX…

After a few high-production and extremely cringy videos I tell Max I'll think about it. We try to practice, but it's all off, so we end it early. Kierra gives me a ride home; she's grumpy the whole way and rants about how Ghost Trick One bought her 20k followers.

"Just look at the dismal engagement," she says,

"Max is blinded by ass again."

I'm mostly silent, processing the idea of collaborating with an artist like her. Max says she's supposed to be funny, but that's not an excuse for poor execution.

The production quality was good, though. Could we make it work? How bad could it be if she just has a verse on one of our songs? Max said we could autotune her beyond recognition, and maybe I could work with her to tighten up her lyrics, explain to her that you shouldn't run with your first draft—if she even writes them down first. Or maybe I could just write her verse for her. Geeeez.

Would it really affect our reputation to work with her? If the song ends up being good it shouldn't matter, right?

And I'm still thinking about it as I lay on my couch alone in my living room, the last slivers of golden light from the sunset seeping into my dark apartment. I'd be able to think a lot better if Jane wasn't making noise as usual. It's not the usual racket though, she's been sobbing and crying like someone died for the past half hour, and it's not a scene for her channel, I checked. What's making her sob like that? Does it have anything to do with that guy who was knocking on her door all night when I first moved in? Did she see my note?

My curiosity gets the better of me, and I remove the photo from the wall and take a peek through the peephole. Jane's sitting on a stool in the middle of the living room. She's hunched over with her head in her hands, wearing a thin white tank top and cut-off jean shorts. Her arms are covered in red. It's not blood, it's paint—a rolling cart of art supplies is next to her and she faces three large canvases. She looks so sad, like a crumpled puppet in a dumpster. She wails, and it makes me cringe; my heart breaks a little.

The paintings are expressionistic portraits of a young and handsome Asian man with a serious expression, but they've been vandalized, slashed by a knife and splattered with red paint. Is this her ex-boyfriend?

She stops crying and collects herself, stumbling into her kitchen to grab her purse. Sniffling, she heads to her front door without changing her clothes or washing the paint off her hands. She's not okay.

I rush out into the hall to meet her, leaving my door open a crack. She's turned away and doesn't notice me behind her. I wave at her. "Jane…"

Jane spins around, she's holding a switchblade and points the blade at me with anger in her bloodshot and mascara-smudged eyes. "Get the hell away from me!"

I jump back. "I just want to talk."

Her hand is trembling, and she's studying my face. Her eyes widen, and she drops her knife. Her hands cover her mouth. "Another one?"

Jane's whole body trembles and a crazed cackle erupts from her. She turns and runs away, leaving with a series of short, sharp screams.

I'm dazed in the aftermath of her emotional outburst and cryptic reaction to me. The lonely knife lays on the ruddy brown carpet. It's beautiful, expensive with a gold inscription on the lacquered wood handle. There's some red paint smudged on it, but I can read the inscription. It says, *"I will always love you."*

Another one… What did she mean by that?

CHAPTER 9

I pull my mail out of the little bronze mailbox in the lobby and look through it as I take the stairs back to my place. On top is a letter from my mom in a pink envelope, with a little smiley face sticker. She's such a sweetheart, it's been too long since we spoke on the phone. I'll call her soon. There's also a piece of junk mail advertising a local pizza place, and two other letters for previous tenants that I'll have to deal with later. The last two aren't mine either—they're Jane's.

One is some sort of card. The envelope is so cheap that I can see the gold-embossed cursive "I'm sorry" through it. The second one is a bill with a threatening bold, red "PAST DUE" stamp on it. Student loans maybe? Medical bills? I'm about to bend over to stick them under her door, but the sound of Kierra wailing out of my apartment sidetracks me. I must have left the door open a crack.

She's on the couch in the fetal position, mascara running down her face. When she sees me, she pathetically opens her arms with a pouty lip, asking for a hug. Just when I thought she'd calmed down. Max is next to her, offering comfort with a back rub. It was a rough morning; I can't blame her. I put the letters down by the door and embrace her. She sobs on my shoulder. "I can't believe he stole my cat."

Max sees my confusion. "It's the name of the car part, catalytic converter."

There's a loud creak as she collapses back on the couch next to them. "It's just, he's never stolen something from me before. Nothing big. A couple twenties from my purse, but nothing like this. It's gotten so bad. What can I even do?"

"You gotta move out of there; it's not healthy," Max says. "You've tried to help him. He's not your responsibility; he's an adult."

"So he can ruin Mom's house like he ruined my fucking Jeep? My fucking Jeep!"

Kierra's mom's house is pretty much already ruined, the lawn is completely overgrown with tall grass and is full of junk, the windows are cracked, every inch of paint is peeling, and it seems like something new has fallen off every time I visit. Her brother and his meth-buddies have completely trashed it, and before her mom died the place was already falling apart due to lack of upkeep. It's depressing, and it's no wonder she avoids home.

Max gently shushes her. "Your car's not ruined, you just need a new cat. You have insurance, right?"

"But they said I have to file a police report or they won't give me any money. I can't turn my own baby brother in. What kind of sister would I be?"

I wish I knew what to say, but I don't, so I just join them on the couch, making a Kierra sandwich with Max. "I'm so sorry, Kierra."

"He's not a bad guy. He's actually a really good guy. He's just sick. It's, like, a disease, right?" She sniffles and breaks into a wail again. "Fucking meth!"

I get her a glass of water, and when I come back Max has changed the subject to cheer her up. They have that boyish excitement in their voice. "And there's going to be karaoke! And signature cocktails!"

"Oooh."

"Ghost's party?" I say as I hand Kierra the drink. "You need to hydrate, babe."

"Yeah, you guys are going to love it. And I think you'll like her too, she's really sweet."

Max's distraction must have worked because Kierra makes mischievous eyes at me from over the glass of water and says, "Can we bring dates? Can Lenora bring a date?"

"You mean Ryan? It's not like we're an item. The kiss was probably just a one-time thing."

Her eyes are fully dry now. "You're hot for him."

A little annoying, but it means she's feeling better, and I can't help but laugh. "And you're not? Vicarious much?"

My phone rings in my bag that hangs by the door, but it stops as soon as I reach it. Jane's mail is right there. "I'll be right back, I need to return some of Jane's mail."

Max perks up like a golden retriever. "You got Jane's mail? Anything interesting?"

Are they really so obsessed with her? Watching The Jane Show is warping their brain. "Oh my god Max, it's just mail. Don't get any ideas."

Stepping out, I catch a woman disappearing up the stairwell like she's being chased. I swear that was Jane's friend with the ponytail. What is she doing here again? Does she live here?

I sprint to the stairwell and get a better look at her as she rushes up out of sight. Where is she going so fast? Almost tripping over myself, I follow her up the next flight of stairs. She's athletic; I can't keep up! Another flight of stairs, and another. "Wait!"

There's one more before I'm halted in my tracks. The stairwell ends at a boarded-up door. This must be the presidential suite that's being renovated, but it doesn't look like a grand entrance, maybe it's the backdoor. Jane's friend must have gone down the last hall. But the hall is empty. Where the hell did she go? I'm sweating so hard that I almost wipe my forehead with Jane's mail. I need to get back in the gym.

A muffled knocking sound comes out from the other side of that weird door. It fills me with a bolt of anxiety, and I sneak back up the stairs to see if I can get a better idea of what it is. Is someone inside? Renovating the apartment? The smell of paint thinner, they must be. Why is the door boarded up and not just locked? I drop Jane's mail, and run my hands across the boards, jiggling them to see how secure they are.

Roaches scatter out from under the boards and behind the door, and I scream, pull my hands away and jump back. Fuck! This apartment has roaches? I can't have roaches again!

There's a stinging pain in my left hand, a fresh, jagged wound across my middle finger. I must have snagged it on a nail. Blood oozes out of the cut, and the pain rises, encompassing my whole hand.

It hurts! And the blood keeps flowing out, dripping down my arm. I must have hit a blood vessel or something. It's running all over the hallway carpet! I squeeze it with my other hand to try to stop the bleeding, and yelp in pain at the sudden pressure on my tender torn flesh. Did someone hear me? I can't pay for carpet cleaning. There's blood on my fucking blouse too! I love this blouse. And Jane's mail that I left on the floor, it's covered in bright red splatters. How am I going to return it now?

CHAPTER 10

Ghost Trick One knows how to throw a party, I'll give her credit for that. It's got an interactive LED dance floor, a dope DJ playing the perfect dance music in a fog-blasting, UFO-shaped booth, the caterers are dressed up like space aliens serving themed appetizers (Xenomorph Wings and Space Slug Sliders), and there's an open bar with signature cocktails like Alien Love Juice and Quantum Drive Jet Fuel. Kierra and I cheers with our cups of Alien Love Juice. It tastes like something a goddess would drink. "This cocktail is…out of this world." I giggle.

Kierra nods. "Yeah, this is good, it has to be top shelf." She peeks behind the bar station, the bartender left his post so there's no one to stop her from grabbing a bottle of Grey Goose and taking a closer look. She's two seconds away from stashing it in her oversized purse.

"Kierra! Lenora!" says an unfamiliar voice. We turn to see Ghost Trick One hanging off Max, her fingers slipped under their crisp, white button up, open at the top to show some chest. Max is wearing a wtf are you doing expression.

Kierra freezes, holding the bottle. "I-I-I thought it was free!"

Ghost laughs. "For Kierra of Totally Toxic? Yeah, it's free! Take two. I can have a case sent to your house if you want. You're my absolute favorite."

Max shakes their head.

The bottle continues its journey into Kierra's purse and she points at Ghost. "I like you."

"You must be Ghost Trick One," I say, offering my hand. "Love this party!"

"Thanks, call me Ghost. I'm a huge fan," she says, leaning in to shake my hand without leaving Max's side. "I'm delighted you could make it. You're having a good time, right?"

We are and let her know it. But then Kierra soon steps on the vibe by saying, "So, are you a rapper or a singer?" The girl's already tipsy…

Ghost demurs at our drummer's question that

probably came out a little more mean-girl than she intended. "So, uh…I guess I'm trying to do something a little different—like in between singing and spoken word."

Kierra pulls a xenomorph wing off a server's tray and shoves it into her mouth. "It's feeling like you should stick to singing."

"You think so? I took singing lessons with Elmar Glass—y'know the celebrity singing coach—and he said I was literally tone deaf."

"You could be great with just a little autotune." Did that come out wrong? I'm genuinely trying to be helpful, but maybe I shouldn't have said that.

But Ghost takes it like we're talking shop. "Really? You think so? Isn't using autotune a little…amateur?"

"No, not at all, babe," Max says, nuzzling up against her closer, their hand definitely inching toward her ass.

She's totally more humble than I expected, not a diva. A little clueless…but workable. "Everyone in the industry uses it, even if they don't talk about it. All the famous singers."

"Really? Even you?" Ghost says to me.

Autotune is not my style, so I avoid the question. "It can be a stylistic choice too—to go with your cool sci-fi aesthetic."

She pauses to think about it. "Yea, I could see that. Maybe we could try it for our song together?"

The moment is awkward. Ghost laughs and breaks the tension with her easy smile. "No pressure! Sorry, I know we haven't agreed on anything yet. You guys should come to my studio and check it out. Record a song on your own—maybe that new one, *Fraud Bitches*. If you like the studio, and want to keep using it, we can talk about a collaboration."

We shrug and agree, there's no losing there. Max whispers something in Ghost's ear and nuzzles up closer. She laughs. "It was really nice to meet you." And they run off together toward the house. Their clothes won't be staying on much longer. Ryan pops into my head. I keep thinking about him, and that kiss. I almost wish he was here.

"Let's do karaoke in the pink crystal cave!" Kierra says, raising her glass before gulping the rest.

On the plastic pink crystal stage, Kierra and I sing *You Oughta Know* by Alanis Morissette, switching off on lines of the verse. Our chemistry is electric, and it's not long before a small crowd gathers. God, I love a crowd. I make eye contact with this guy who has a gorgeous Adrian Brody nose and that soft intense, brooding charisma. Usually I'd be drooling over him, but ever since Ryan and I made out the night of the show

I've been less boy-crazy. God, does that mean I'm…Ryan-crazy?

After Max (lipstick collar, hickeys and all) drops us off at my place, Kierra and I keep the party going with the vodka Ghost gifted her and some leftover orange juice.

"Schwoo-dwivas!" she says gleefully and licks the dinner knife that mixed our drinks.

We enjoy our beverages together on either side of the couch, facing one another with our legs casually intertwined.

Sometimes you're just looking for someone to give you bad advice. And when that's the case, Kierra is a reliable option. I sigh deeply before confessing my horniness in the form of a question. "It'd be stupid to sleep with Ryan, right?"

"Um…actually that's a GENIUS move? Have you seen that man? Honestly, I can't understand why you haven't hit that yet," Kierra says, and catches my eyes over a swig of her drink.

I blush. "He's practically my landlord, and he lives next door. It's playing with fire."

"Uh, yeah. Playing with fire is fun, that's why people do it."

Is she forgetting that he might not know I'm trans? "But—"

"Lenora, if you don't fuck him tonight I will!" She kicks me playfully and I hop up in mock outrage. He's probably not even awake, he said he sleeps early and deeply, but I'm stumbling down the hallway to his door already. Is there the smell of paint thinner in the hallway again? I feel dizzy. How many drinks did I have? I try to brace my body against the wall but lose my footing, tripping over myself and crashing into his door. The door opens, and I'm in his arms. "Oh, hi—"

He smiles down at me, the sexual tension thick between us. "Lenora! Long night?"

My arms reach around his neck, and he grabs me by the waist and pulls me in, shutting the door behind us. His sparsely decorated living room is a blur, and we're in the bedroom, our hands all over each other, our lips meeting the other's flesh. He's massaging my breasts over my tube top and kissing my neck. God, I love it, he's good at this. I feel a warm, tingling sensation all throughout my body, and I'm practically whimpering. "Please fuck me."

He stops, sobering. "We shouldn't. I don't want to take advantage of you."

My hands slide over his huge bulge, squeezing it through his jeans. "Please, I want it."

His eyes roll back into his head, and he gasps. "O…kay."

I touch myself as he unbuttons his pants and reveals his member. My god—it deserves its own zip code. The sight of it makes my tuck come undone.

Before I can panic, Ryan grins at my bulge. "Oh wow, I see we've got company."

It turns out he's okay with me being trans and still having my original equipment. He's curious and explores it with his mouth. He's getting really into it now, blowing me like he's worshiping it. His devotion sets off a small alarm bell, but it feels so good, so I push the feeling away and let him take me deeper. Or maybe he's just having fun, he lets me slide it between his ass cheeks. I can feel his asshole loosening, he's so relaxed.

"Put it in me," he moans. And with those words I slide it in slowly. It feels good to penetrate someone so strong. I'm in and out and he moans again with pleasure, but pulls away and turns around. "My turn."

I'm eager for his cock and flip over, exposing my ass to him. "Fuck me."

He enters me and sends me to another dimension, fucking me into oblivion. I cum again and again until he's finished. The feeling of his strong arms manipulating my body and his hardness deep inside me is exhilarating.

Ryan's cock slides out of me, and I flop onto the bed next to him, my insides relaxing to fill the gap he left behind, his cum dripping from my hole. I close my eyes, and my body settles into the delicious post-orgasm sinking, every muscle relaxing. My brain was completely fucked out of my skull, and there's only the blissful emptiness of being a satisfied body.

"This was a mistake."

My eyes open, my brain shoots back, and my body tenses up. I'm fully alert. "What?"

His voice is monotone and his expression is completely blank. He looks at me with dead eyes. "I'm sorry, but you should go."

I shake my head and get dressed as fast as I can. Again. I thought he was different. I pass the threshold of his bedroom door and hear him say behind me, "Don't tell anyone about this."

He's just like all of the other fucking chasers. Tears are starting to form in my eyes. I swing open his apartment door, but it stops when it hits someone standing in the hall. It's that incel neighbor from the unit across mine. Was he standing outside Ryan's door the whole time? Was he listening? He's almost right up against me and looks down with those creepy half-frightened eyes and sniffs. "I-I-I was—"

"Get away from me you creep!" I say and push him out of the way.

Kierra is snoring on the couch when I run into my

apartment and slam the door behind me. I guess it could have been worse. At least he didn't get violent. People who act on behalf of their penis are dangerous when they get what they want.

I flop on the bed and pull the covers up to my chest. The room looks alien, like creatures could be lurking in the dark corners. Jane's knife gleams on my nightstand, the golden inscription catching the lamplight. I cut the light, shut my eyes, and fall into unconsciousness before I can cry myself to sleep.

CHAPTER 11

"Jane kind of looks like you, doesn't she?"

I push Kierra away from the peephole. Jane's in leather, strutting around one of her streaming partners who's on his knees, almost in a prayer position. His head is bulbous and fleshy and shining, like he's wearing some sort of mask. She grins and flips back her braids and snaps the leather whip in her hand. She *does* look like me. How could I never have noticed this before? Isn't she white? And kind of chubby? But she's the spitting image of me.

Was her apartment always this huge? It looks cavernous inside—the ceilings are high and the room is open. There are chains draped across the exposed beams of the ceiling like party streamers, and her rug lies on a concrete floor instead of the hardwood floor I remember.

A dim light turns on to reveal that the performance isn't for a camera, there's a small crowd of men on metal folding chairs, their faces shrouded by darkness. They're shifting in their seats, their erections pushing against their matching khaki pants with anticipation.

I look down at the man on his knees, he's wearing a baby mask, frozen in a crying expression. The smooth stiffness of the leather whip feels good on my palms. I lash the whip across his back. It makes a satisfying red welt upon his pale flesh. I take off his mask—it's Ronald, my old roommate's boyfriend. The crowd of men gasp and moan, and I laugh and put my hands on his cheeks. I lift his head, and it tears at the neck from his torso like pulling off a piece of cotton candy. His face melts into bliss and his exposed spine twists and writhes like an earthworm.

I'm outside now, standing in tall, dry grass, surrounded by gnarled trees, young and bare. I'm not sure how I got here. The sky is clear and blue, speckled with beaming clouds. Not far from me is Jane, she looks like herself again, wearing the same outfit I first saw her in. Her back is to me, and she stands on a short concrete wall—it's the threshold of a dam. I recognize it, this is the dam that my friends and I would sneak off to in high school, where we'd hop the fence and smoke weed and hook up. I've stood on that threshold before, feeling the thrill of looking down at the 80-foot drop, the rush of my teenage sense of invincibility clashing with the knowledge that taking my own life would be so easy.

I step toward Jane. "Jane, don't. I just want to talk."

She turns her head, and I glimpse her profile. I don't think I ever realized how beautiful her face is, the strong and soft features perfectly blending into each other. She's been crying. "He never loved me. He wouldn't even bring me home."

Jane walks forward off the drop, her arms lifting in the gravity of the fall. I scream, "No!" and run toward the edge. Her body is twisted and broken on the sidewalk below, the sidewalk in front of our apartment building. Blood pours from her mouth and her dead eyes stare up at me.

I wake up, covered in vodka-tinged sweat, still smelling like last night's sex. My head pounds. What time is it? I find my phone under the bed, and there's a text from an unknown number. "Sorry I've been a bad neighbor. I'll keep it down at night."

Jane. I push away the dream-image of her broken body and text her back. "It's okay. I have your knife btw."

She replies right away, "keep it" and I wonder if

she's next-door, also lying in bed with a hangover.

I have coffee at home, but I can't stand the thought of the loud electric coffee grinder, and the effort to make it, with this headache. So, it's off to the shitty coffee place down the street. I'm not sure where my phone is, but coffee comes first, so I roll out of bed and put on a serviceable outfit.

Kierra isn't here, but she left a note: "Didn't want to wake you sleeping off all of the AMAZING SEX I'm sure you had last night. Gotta deal with some of Michael's bullshit at the house, text me later I want all of the juicy deets xoxo."

The note makes me cringe. I love Kierra, but I just want to forget last night.

When I step out and lock up, I'm faced with that goddamned flyer—it's pinned to my front door. It's crusty, and my eyes in the picture are crossed out with deranged Sharpie scribbles, and the word BITCH is furiously written over the show info. I tear it off my door and crumple it up, pushing down a desperate sadness rising in my chest. Who did this?

I didn't leave it all behind. I'll never leave it behind.

A latch clicks, and I freeze, knowing I'm going to have to deal with the person I want to see least in the world.

"Good morning, Lenora!" Ryan says cheerfully like last night didn't happen.

I turn away from him to my door and avert my eyes, crumpling the flyer more in my hands, hoping he'll leave me alone.

"I SAID, 'Good morning, Lenora.'"

"What do you want," I reply in almost a whisper.

"Just a neighborly greeting, is that too much?"

My face is hot, twisted with disgust, and I peer up at him. "After last night?"

"What're you talking about?" He's so bad at playing dumb.

"After you fucked me, and I fucked you, and you—"

He punches the door above my head. It rattles against its hinges with an echoing bang. I gasp and shrink against the smooth painted wood under his seething breath. Both of his arms are above me against the wall, creating a cage. "Don't lie, Lenora. You know what happens to lying girls, don't you? Nothing happened last night. Say it."

I try not to whimper but fail. "Nothing happened."

"That's right you little freak. I know your dirty secret. Don't play games with me, this is *my* property. And I could have you on the street whenever I want— sleeping in a dirty tent and eating trash like the subhuman garbage clogging up the sidewalks, is that what you want?"

"No," I say in a whisper.

"Good girl." He walks off, head held high, his keyring jangling with every step.

CHAPTER 12

The hot streams of water from the shower feel good running down my back, cutting the jitters of the creepy encounter I just had with Ryan. I already felt dirty from the party and sex, and seeing Ryan's unhinged chaser behavior gave me a deep sense of filth that covers every inch of my body. He's not who I thought he was, who he presented himself to be. This man is dangerous, and he violated me. I should have seen the signs, but he seemed so genuine. Are my instincts shot?

I'm almost shaking and when I grab the bar of soap it squirts out of my hand and slides across the bathroom floor. I step out of the clawfoot tub, careful not to slip, and bend down to pick it up. The grout on the tile wall has degraded. Was it like this when I moved in?

Moisture could get trapped in there, and I'd have to deal with a mold problem, again. But it's just the one tile, the grout on the others isn't breaking apart...that's strange.

The tile loosens when I jiggle it until it pops off. It has cords attached to the other side, some sort of electronics fixed on it. Is this a fucking camera? The hole left behind goes all the way into Ryan's apartment! The surface does have a slightly different quality than the rest of the tiles if I look at it from a certain angle. It's a hidden camera for sure...pointed right at the toilet! That creep has been watching me shit?

I hop up, almost slipping, and cover myself with a towel. It's a struggle to put clothes on my still damp body, but I get dressed as fast as I can. With the flashlight from my junk drawer, I check every tile in the bathroom to see if it's semi-translucent. There are at least three that are suspicious, and who knows how many more hidden cameras are in my apartment. I hear a muffled voice talking through the wall. Ryan is home, and he's talking to someone in his apartment or maybe he's on the phone. If he's been checking the cameras in the past fifteen minutes, he knows I've discovered them. Or he'll see that I removed a tile from the other side. I rush to fit the tile back in place and try to steady my breath. This is no time to panic.

I need to text Max and Kierra. Where the fuck is

my phone? I search frantically, and it's under my bed, completely drained of battery. My hands tremble and I struggle to plug it into the charger on the nightstand.

The front door of Ryan's apartment slams. I feel his every step in the hallway. Is he going to come in? I run to my front door and latch the chain lock, and look through the peephole into the hall. He walks by and I swear I glimpse the expression of a psychopath. The footsteps stop, and there's a knock next-door. Jane.

She's letting him in!

I almost rush out of my apartment to warn her, but he's already in, and I don't know what to do. Instead, I knock Snowball off the wall and look into the peephole. God, I hope he doesn't hurt her. He can't hurt her.

Jane is in a work outfit—naked with leather straps tight around her body, studded with metal loops, making her curves spill out of the cross sections it creates. Her camera and lighting is set up. Ryan strips down and puts on a realistic wolf mask—he's the wolf guy from her videos!

Jane's talking to him, maybe giving instructions, she seems frustrated. She's angry saying something about "Crystal." Is that her friend? He seems almost angry too, but mechanical.

She throws her hands up in frustration and turns to her laptop on the chair, bending over to do something on it, exposing her ass. Before she can turn back around, Ryan grabs her from her waist, picks her up, and flips her around in the air, catching her legs over his arms. Her eyes are wide, and when she recovers from the shock she starts hitting him with her palms, looking more annoyed now than scared. Her voice is muffled, but it sounds like she's yelling, "I haven't started it yet!"

I can almost see his sadistic smile under the wolf mask as his cock stands up straight. He plunges into her, and she screams out with the violence of being forcibly entered with no lubrication. Terrified cries reverberate through the wall, each one causing panic to rise in me and my breaths to become quicker.

Jane squirms and hits and desperately tries to strangle him and pull his mask off, but Ryan is too strong. She eventually stops struggling and her body goes limp, her head falling back and bobbing with each thrust. Blood runs down her thighs. He grunts like an animal.

Ryan carries her limp body toward the peephole, still inside her, and slams her head against the wall, causing the view to go black. I jump back and cover my mouth to stop my scream, but a horrified moan still escapes my throat. Did he hear me?

He's banging her head against the wall again and again. Harder and harder, her defeated moaning becoming quieter with each strike until the sounds stop. Does he know about the peephole? Is he doing this for me?

Terrible silence. I can't look, but I have to. Jane's corpse lies on the floor of her apartment. Her face is bloody and mangled. The maw of Ryan's wolf mask is stained red. He killed her. He fucking murdered Jane.

CHAPTER 13

He's dragging Jane's corpse across the hallway, I'm watching him do it from my front door through the peephole, holding my breath. Ryan takes her into his apartment and slams the door. I have to get out of here. I have to get out now.

I grab my purse hanging by the door. In the hall, the creepy across-the-way neighbor is poking his head out of his unit looking back and forth. He must have heard or seen something too. The sound of keys jingle, and the lock on Ryan's door clicks. He's coming out into the hall!

I push past my neighbor and into his apartment, shutting the door behind us before Ryan can see me. The man across the hall is creepy, but probably harmless, and I need to hide. That homicidal maniac Ryan is after me next, I just know it. I don't think he saw me go in, but he definitely heard the door close.

The creepy neighbor sniffs and stares down at me. Hushed and panicked I say, "Hide me! I need to hide."

He nods, and I rush into the first open door and shut myself into what must be his bedroom. His walls are plastered with explicit porn posters and print outs of trans women, proudly displaying their dicks and opening their holes for the camera. Some of them are covered in cum, giving blowjobs or being spit-roasted. They're covered with disgusting slogans like "chicks with dicks," "shemale fantasy," "tranny whores," "futanari," and "the best of both worlds."

Poppers and dildos and dirty magazines litter the floor. And the bed—the bed is absolutely covered in hyper-realistic sex dolls. Their tits are cartoonishly huge, they're dressed in skimpy outfits, and some have their unrealistically massive, fake penises exposed, sticking out of tacky lingerie. I almost gag imagining him molesting these poor dolls. This guy is a certified incel chaser-freak. Maybe I'm not safer here.

There's a loud knock on his front door. Is Ryan going to come in? The closet is blocked by a massive pile of dirty clothes so I turn off the light and worm my way into the pile of sex dolls—there must be half a dozen—I cover myself as much as possible to blend in. Fuck! My phone isn't in my bag, it must still be on my nightstand. But my fresh canister of pepper spray gel is. I grip it tight, and my finger rests on the trigger. Be steady, girl. Don't panic.

The neighbor is talking to Ryan in the next room, but I can't make out what they're saying. My palms are sweating around the pepper spray gel. God, I hope he doesn't come in.

The muffled conversation stops, and a door closes. Did Ryan leave or close the door behind him? The bedroom door creaks open, and I hold my breath and become as still and as silent as the dolls on the bed. The voice I hear isn't Ryan's. "He's gone. I told him you ran down the stairs and left the building."

I emerge from the tangle of synthetic limbs and breathe a sigh of relief. "Thank god."

"I've been…concerned about you. That's why I was outside his door last night. My name's Dale."

I'm not sure if I believe Creepy Dale, the dude is clearly a major pervert. "Do you think he left?"

"I do. I'm sure of it."

Do I risk going back to my apartment to get my phone? He could be waiting for me there, or at the main entrance downstairs. I need help, I need to call someone. The cops? They've never helped me before, but they'd have to protect me from a rampaging killer, wouldn't they? Probably not. Maybe I should just deal with this whacked-out creep and his pile of fuck-dolls and stay here until I can sneak out at night. "Fuck."

He sniffles loudly. "Aren't you...aren't you going to thank me?"

I look up at Creepy Dale. He's blushing hot through his pale skin, snot running down his nose, and his hard-on fully visible under his thin, stained sweatpants. Totally Toxic show flyers with my face on them are posted on the wall behind him, mixed in with the porn cut-outs. "I saved you. You owe me."

I'm dumbfounded. He reaches toward my chest with a shaky hand. I instinctively slap his hand away, and pull the trigger, covering his eyes with the spicy blue gel. He reaches for his face, screaming, but in a weird hoarse hyperventilating way, like a child imitating a velociraptor. And he falls to the floor, writhing in the fetal position. It's way creepier than a normal scream, but I'm grateful it isn't too loud; he would have given me away with a manly yell. That was impulsive—I wasn't thinking.

I sneak into my apartment, checking corners where predators could hide, praying Dale was right about Ryan leaving. My phone is still on my nightstand like I thought, and it must be charged enough to use now. But something's off. Wasn't Jane's knife next to it when I left? It's not here.

Strong arms wrap around my body in a vise grip, and I drop my pepper spray. Ryan body-slams me into the bed and turns me around to face him while putting the entire force of his weight against me. I struggle, trying to break free of his grip and reach for my phone on the nightstand. His large hand presses against my face, shoving my head into the mattress and causing pain to shoot down my neck.

He's so heavy, I can barely breathe. His fingers pry open my mouth, poking me in the eye and tearing the insides of my lip. I close my eyes and can feel his erection pressing against me; it makes me gag. A plastic vial touches my lips, and my eyes shoot open. His grin is stretched wide, and his eyes are like a wild animal, droplets of his spit hit my face with his excited breathing. I want to spit out the liquid he's pouring down my throat, but he holds my mouth open and I can't. Whatever was in that vial is inside me now.

I scream, and he covers my mouth with his palm and presses his weight against me further. My right arm is freed, and I reach for his eyes, but he takes it and twists, causing pain to sear into my shoulder. He tucks it underneath him and puts his hand back over my mouth. The strong arms that once made me feel protected are now squeezing the life out of me like a python. I wriggle and twist with all my strength, but it's not enough, he's too strong. I'm totally crushed, and I can barely breathe. It's hopeless.

He's drugged me. But it hasn't taken effect yet, so maybe I can use that to my benefit. Maybe he messed up the dose, gave me too little. I slow my breathing and weaken my struggling and act dazed, doing my best to look like I'm passing out. My muffled screams fade, and I let my body go completely limp and relax my eyelids so that they fall open a crack, exposing the whites of my eyes. He notices, and his grip on me loosens just a little.

His biceps relax. Patience. I have to time this perfectly. He shakes me, and gives me a slap, but I resist reacting or tensing my body. Ryan finally lets go of me and gets off the bed. Is this my chance?

He takes my thumb and places it on my phone. Fuck, he's unlocked it. But I can't move now, it's too soon. I feel it again, and then nothing for a while. I peek from my playing-dead position, barely opening my eyes. This bastard is going through my phone, he probably turned the passcode off.

Ryan's not facing me, so I get up as slowly and quietly as I can. When he looks up from my phone I bolt, trying to pick up the pepper spray but fumbling and dropping it. It rolls across the room, and Ryan seems to have registered that I'm mid-escape. I turn to run, but I'm stumbling. I'm lightheaded, and I can't think clearly. Whatever he gave me is kicking in. If I can just get to the door, maybe someone can help me. Maybe, if I'm loud enough, someone will come. "Help me! Help!"

I reach my unit's front door and grasp the knob with both hands, steadying myself, trying not to fall. My head is spinning. The door slams against the wall when I throw it open, and I'm running down the hall to escape. Maybe someone could even hear me from the street if I scream loud enough. "Please, someone help!"

But my balance is terrible, and I trip over my feet, face-planting onto the carpet of the second-floor hallway. I try to lift myself up, but I'm so dizzy and tired. It feels like I'm falling through the floor. Elbows buckle and I collapse, not even able to crawl.

No. I can't let this happen. I lift myself up to my hands and knees again. A hand scoops me up from my shoulder, and I gasp as I'm flipped over on to my back. Ryan and red-eyed Dale stare down at me as I slip away into the darkness that fills my vision.

CHAPTER 14

My feet drag across the carpet. My arms draped around their necks; I'm being carried by Ryan and Dale down the hall. Head heavy, limbs heavy, can't move; my muscles are so weak, I'm nearly completely paralyzed. Brain is foggy and vision blurs in and out. They drag me into the broken elevator—he said it was broken—and Ryan inserts a key into the bronze panel of buttons and presses the one with the faded label that reads "Presidential Suite." They're taking me upstairs…for what? I need to run, I need to fight, but I'm so weak. We were supposed to record with Ghost Trick One tomorrow… The band is counting on me. How long will they keep me? How long will I be gone? Ghost is going to think I'm flaky… Are they going to kill me? And I was actually starting to look forward to the recording session. And now...wait a minute, I just got fucking kidnapped. Focus girl, don't let the drugs completely mess you up, you're not going out like this.

The elevator stops with a jolt, we're at the top floor. The doors open directly to the presidential suite, and I'm taken in. The suite takes up the whole floor and looks like it hasn't been touched since the 20s, 30s, whatever... Musty, the smell of rot and chemicals—that chemical smell—is thick in the air, and I almost throw up. Dead potted plants, the original furniture. Plaster chunks from the ceiling are scattered all over the dirty, faded carpet, it has a garish pattern. It's dark, low lighting from a few bare lamps and tarnished chandeliers. The windows have been boarded up, the original, tattered, dark green curtains barely hang on.

In the living room—did they call it the parlor back then? Part of the room is blocked out with slightly transparent plastic curtains, the dimness causing the objects inside to be only silhouettes. The rest of the room looks like it hasn't been touched either, there's peeling wallpaper, the walls lined with wood trim. Will Max and Kierra know I'm gone? Leather couches split open, their stuffing spilling out. Ryan has my phone... The head of a bear snarling mounted to the wall. He'll probably text them and say it's me.

Large dark stains all over the carpet and a brick fireplace. Ornately carved wooden chairs, a man sits in one. His face is shadowed, he has a cigarette in his grin. In the chair across from him is one of those realistic trans sex dolls that Dale had. Max will know something's wrong…won't they? A broken grand piano, the cover smashed in, another sex doll sits at the bench as if it is playing. But how will they know where I am? A dirty bare mattress on the floor, a young boy cuddles up to a doll on it.

My head flops to one side, and I catch a glimpse into another room through an open doorway. It's full of TV monitors showing hidden camera feeds in the building. A man touches himself as he watches, the blue glow of the monitors reflecting in his glasses. There are other girls on there, their private moments being invaded. Flies stuck in a web, and they don't even know it.

With a few jerks, I'm pulled into the master bedroom. The door slams behind us; it's huge. The wallpaper is completely peeled off, the plaster is so damaged that the brick is showing through. A large broken mirror on a wooden dresser. How am I going to get out of here? Am I going to die here, in this disgusting room? No. I can't, not here, not like this.

The upholstered headboard of the bed is covered in

dark stains, and its stuffing is bursting out. The light-colored sheets are soaked in a massive puddle of blood, and lying in the puddle is Jane—Jane's corpse, battered and blue, her hair a tangled mess and her face smashed. But her eyes are open, and a sliver of light seeps through two of the boards covering the window. It illuminates her irises—ice blue, brighter than I'd ever seen when she was alive, she's still so beautiful. Another man sits beside her, stroking her hair and looks up. It's the pigman from her streams, mask and all. Chains hang from the wall above the bed, anchored into the brick.

The master bath is separated only by open curtains, the entrance is large and there's a clawfoot tub positioned as a centerpiece. The tiled floor is encrusted with mold, and I don't want to know what else. They're going to kill me, like they killed Jane. Ryan and Dale lift me up from the legs and carefully place me into the tub. They handcuff me to the spigot attached to the wall. I need to get out of here. But my body is completely limp. If I still have muscles, I've forgotten how to use them.

My head rolls to the side, and I look at Jane on the bed. That can't be me; I can't let that be me. I try to summon the strength to move my body, but instead darkness encloses my vision again.

Through a blur, I see that Jane's body has been stripped of all her clothing. It's moving, and her limbs jostle stiffly against the bloody sheets with the rhythmic thrusting of Dale. He's naked too, his pasty skin almost glowing in the low light. He's fucking her corpse. I can't believe it. This has to be a dream—but I know it isn't. The pigman, still wearing his mask—does he ever take it off?—walks up to the bedside, he's naked, erect. He has some sort of saw, and he digs the blade into her neck, causing stale blood to dribble. He steadies her head by pressing it into the mattress as he saws. "Her head is mine."

Dale thrusts harder into her, squealing and huffing. He grabs her penis. "I…I want her…girldick."

Pigman chuckles and saws into her neck harder— he must be reaching the spine; the sound has changed to a grinding. "Making the best of a bad situation. She was never up to standard. She was botched before we even got to her."

There's a popping and tearing as he lifts her severed head up off her body. He raises it to Dale's eye level, and in a high-pitched mocking tone says, "Kiss me."

Ryan is sitting in the darkness at the back of the room, on his phone; he looks bored. Dale tongues Jane's caved in mouth, going unnaturally deep due to her broken jaw, getting the leftover viscera all over his face. As he cries out in orgasm, I puke over the side of the tub. I heave and tears pour out of my eyes—that's going to be me if I can't get out of here. I'm locked up in a den of serial killers.

Pigman laughs and turns Jane's head toward me, wiggling it in the air before he lowers it to his erection. This can't be happening—my head swims and I clasp my eyes shut as they roll back into my head, and I collapse into the tub. I'm sinking.

CHAPTER 15

Where am I? No longer in the tub. My arms are spread and stretched above me, tightly bound with chains wrapped around and around. I'm on the bed, chained to the wall, lying in the damp bloodstained sheets where Jane was, stripped down to my underwear. Light is no longer seeping out of the boarded-up windows, and it's hard to see, but once my eyes adjust, I can tell that I'm alone in the room. How much time has passed?

I struggle against the chains, moving my body back and forth to see if I can wriggle out but they don't budge. They're held in place with two padlocks on each side. At least I can move my body again; the drugs are wearing off. But how am I going to get out? Am I really alone? It no longer feels like it. Is that a face? Someone's watching me?

No. It's Jane's severed head. They placed it on an old end table in the corner of the room, facing me on the bed. I scream. "Help me! Help me!"

The door opens and Ryan comes in. His face is emotionless. "Save your energy, Lenora. No one can hear you up here."

I let out a cry of frustration and sob, my tears stain my face, my mascara stings my eyes. "Please, let me go. Don't hurt me."

"I'm not going to hurt you. Not if you cooperate. I only want the best for you."

"You killed Jane!"

Ryan grins and flashes Jane's knife. He waves it in the air in front of my face. "Jane was nothing. You, Lenora, are a goddess. You're perfect, and we're going to help you shine like the goddess you are."

He's completely mad. He brings the blade close to my chest but doesn't touch it. "Did your other boyfriend give you this knife, you little slut?" He reads the inscription *I will always love you* in a disgusted tone. "I knew you were unfaithful, you dirty girl."

Another man comes into the room and Ryan closes the blade and puts it in his back pocket. It's a tall white guy wearing an Indian-styled shirt and harem pants—some sort of poser hippy fuckboy. His jaw is chiseled and lined with stubble; I'd think he was hot if I saw him on the street. He puts his hand on Ryan's shoulder.

"She's radiant. And she's intact?"

Ryan smiles. "Yes, and it's magnificent."

Soon all of the men are at the foot of the bed, Ryan's entire warped crew. Dale, hippy guy, pigman, babyman (I can recognize him without his mask because of his cheesy tattoos), and another man I recognize—a short guy with dark spiky hair and a golden-brown complexion who also lives in the apartment complex. They inspect my body without touching it and make noises of approval, some almost orgasmic. I can feel their hot breath, making my skin crawl, they're inhaling over me, taking in my scent.

"She's a goddess."

"Perfect body. Perfection."

"The next step of human evolution."

"Tight ass. Look at those gorgeous tits. Are they real?"

"Doll. Like a doll."

"Legs, so smooth."

"Just like this, forever."

"The perfect woman. She's the perfect woman."

"And it's intact."

"I want to see her cock."

"Let's see it. Let's see that dick."

"I want to see it."

"I want to see it."

I let out an exasperated cry. "Stop! I want to talk to Ryan alone. All of you leave! Now!"

The chasers groan in unison and look to Ryan. He nods at them. "I'll take care of this. Just have some patience."

The man in the harem pants steps forward, seeming to speak for the rest of the group. "The oath."

"We share the chosen," Ryan replies in a robotic way. He starts again and the other men join him, chanting together:

"We worship the chosen.

"We bind the chosen.

"We share the chosen.

"We tell no one.

"We say nothing."

And then they shuffle out, whispering about a "rebirth." Ryan looks at me from the door. I plead to him with my eyes. "Come here, babe. Sit with me."

He sits down next to me on the bed, and when he straightens himself against the bounce of the mattress, I see the end of Jane's knife poking out slightly from his back pocket. I stroke his leg with my free foot. "Babe, we don't have to do it like this. Why don't you untie me and we can go down to your apartment. I'll do anything you want."

Ryan's smile is arrogant, like I'm a stupid little girl. "Your place is here. You don't understand yet but what you're about to go through is a great honor."

His vagueness is excruciating. "Please let me go, I'll do anything. Anything. I won't fight. I won't tell anyone about this."

Ryan sighs and starts to get up. I gently block him with my leg, my foot stroking across his jeans over his crotch. His eyes widen in surprise, and he plops back on to the mattress. Jane's knife pokes out of his pocket a little more, and he doesn't seem to notice. "Oh my."

I turn my body slightly and put my other bare foot on his jeans over his cock. With all of the grace I can muster, I stroke around and up and down his member. His arms brace himself on the bed and he moans. I never thought my foot-job skills could save my life one day.

As I stroke and lightly grip him with my toes, Ryan grinds his hips into the bed in rhythm with my pleasuring. With each grind Jane's knife inches out of his pocket more and more. Time to increase the intensity just slightly, and then clamp his penis with my feet, jerking him off to completion. He breathes deeper and deeper and then lets out a loud moan with his orgasm. My stomach churns.

Ryan's orgasm shocks him, and he bolts to his feet.

Hands over his stained jeans, he rushes out and slams and locks the door behind him.

Jane's knife is left behind on the mattress. I maneuver it with my feet on to the floor and kick it underneath the nightstand next to the bed. That will come in handy later. It has to.

CHAPTER 16

"Don't let them do to you…what they did to me," says a woman's hoarse voice, sending a chilling déjà vu down my spine.

My eyes shoot open. I thought I was alone. Who said that? Am I hallucinating? But I recognize the voice. It's Jane. Her head is still on the end table in the corner of the room.

"Jane?"

Jane's head speaks. "Hi, Lenora."

I must be losing my mind. "But…you're dead."

"What tipped you off?"

I cackle, if anyone can keep their sense of humor after having their head cut off, it's a trans woman.

"They'll use you, Lenora. And when they get what

they want, they'll throw you away. Don't let them do it."

"How? How can I escape?"

Jane's voice is raspier now. "They want your body. Their perfect tranny fantasy. That's all they care about. Use that. Ruin it for them, if you have to."

"Ruin my body? I don't understand."

"You know what men want. They're idiots. We've both been in situations like this before."

It doesn't make sense, but what advice would, coming from a dead girl? Jane deserved so much better than this. Tears come to my eyes and I choke back a sob. "Jane...I'm sorry. I should've done something. I should've known you were in trouble."

It almost looks like her bashed-in mouth is smiling. "It's okay, my life sucked. Just one disappointment and goodbye after another, again and again. I'm glad it's done."

My heart sinks even further. "If I had gotten to know you..."

"It's too late for me, Lenora. But not for you. Survive. At all costs. Don't die here. Don't end up like me."

"Who are you talking to?" Ryan says as he enters the room, slamming the door shut.

"Just myself...my sanity escaped days ago," I

reply.

I can't tell if he thinks I'm cracking a joke or what. "Okay."

He searches the room—almost frantically—opening the creaky drawers of the decrepit furniture, looking under the sheets, in the corners, in the bathroom. He must be looking for the knife. I need to distract him.

"What's going to happen to me, Ryan? I'm scared."

He's looking on the ground now. "You'll see, it's nothing to be afraid of."

"But why me?"

He's checking under the bed; he'll look under the nightstand next. And when he does, he'll find the knife. "Because you're perfect, Lenora. We love you just the way you are."

"What're you doing? Are you looking for something?"

Ryan gets up and looks around the room a little more, scratching his head. "Yeah, but I guess it's not here."

He leaves without another word. I must have distracted him, or maybe he looked right at the thing but didn't see it in his frustration. Either way, Jane's knife is still hidden under the nightstand and Ryan doesn't know about it. I still have a chance.

CHAPTER 17

The wind tickles my temples as my mom drives us down a winding country road in her old convertible. It's our time, my brothers have been left behind to fight and play Nintendo. The sky is bright blue with a few beautiful clouds, and the fields of local farms wiz by. Maybe we'll stop for a snack at a drive-thru restaurant as we approach the city. Mom rubs my shoulder and smiles at me. I return the smile and lean back, closing my eyes and smelling the sweet, fragrant air.

    It's been three or four days, maybe longer, since I've been chained up. I'm overdue on my hormone shot, and have barely been given any food—in order to "purify" my body. My underwear and clothes are soiled from not showering and trying to use the bedpan while chained up, only having "help" from Ryan. I haven't been able to shave my legs or armpits. My arms are numb and aching, the chains have loosened some, but the pain hasn't gotten any better.

I'm alive but I don't know for how long. They haven't raped me, but I know that's coming. They're preparing for something. I'm guessing it'll involve each of them taking their turn before they snuff me out.

Pushing to live another day,
pushing up, puh-pushing on,
pushing past and staying strong!
Suck this pain, from my veins
and fill them up with your love,
I want toxic love!

Writing songs in my head, and reliving good memories are the only things keeping me sane. And I've had plenty of time to do both. If I get out of here, the first thing I'm going to do after a shower is get a double veggie burger and fries at that vegan spot on Figueroa.

I'll go with Kierra and Max; we can plan our album. Fill a notebook with song lyrics. I'm sure Ghost will understand, given the circumstances, and give us another shot at recording. Our album is going to be so fucking good, if we can finish it. If I can get out of here. When I get out of here. I have to believe I can get out of here.

I flinch when the door opens and Ryan comes in. He smiles. "We're almost ready for you."

He's so delusional that I've decided playing along is my best chance for survival. I'm weak, and it's hard to muster the energy, but I manage it. "Oh, babe! That's so exciting."

Maybe I laid it on too thick because he looks suspicious. "Really? You're excited?"

"Honestly, I'm nervous. Really nervous. But I trust you, I trust your plan. You said you want the best for me. And I don't really have a choice, do I?" I give my best fake giggle.

"Hah. You're right. You're going to finally reach your true potential, Lenora. And I'm so excited for you."

"So…what do you have planned for me? Just so I can mentally prepare."

His eyes gloss over, and his stare goes through me. "Your rebirth. You'll become the goddess that you are inside. Forever."

I've dated some lunatics in my time, but this guy is on another level. "What…and what's that mean?"

After staring off into space for a few moments, Ryan turns around and closes the door behind him, leaving me alone in the dingy room again.

They've been building something in the parlor, but I don't know what, I hear heavy objects moving and power tools. What is this sick "rebirth" ceremony that they have planned for me? Some sort of ritualistic gang rape? I want to puke.

They keep saying they want me "untouched" and "intact." They're obsessed with me, obsessed with my body. Obsessed with my penis.

No one is coming to save me. I'm on my own, Ryan has been texting my friends, pretending to be me, telling them I'm fine—I just took a surprise trip with a guy I'm dating. I wish I could be more confident that Max and Kierra would know something is seriously wrong—I wouldn't bail on them like that for a guy, I don't think I would—but even if they thought something was up, they don't know where I am. This is the last place they'd think to look. Have they reported me as a missing person? Are other people looking for me too? Or do they just think I'm a lovesick flake?

Ryan enters the room again, holding a reusable grocery bag. "I have some things for you."

God, I hope it's not some sort of torture device. "What are they, babe?"

He lays out the contents next to me on the bed. It's a small makeup set, lingerie, a douching kit, a disposable razor and shaving cream, and some other toiletries. "The room is ready for your rebirth. Tonight. I brought these for you so you can get made up and look sexy for it."

"I can take a shower?" A shower would be heaven. I'm so disgusting and uncomfortable and I need this hair off my legs.

"Yes, you can. I'm going to take off those chains and you can clean yourself, shave, and put on some makeup." He holds up his index finger in warning. "Only if you promise not to try anything. Don't try to escape, you won't make it."

This might be my chance to get Jane's knife. My only chance.

"I won't, I promise. Pinky swear," I say with a convincing giggle.

"I'll be right here to watch you to make sure."

Shit. How can I be alone after he's unchained me, even just for a moment?

"Don't do anything stupid," Ryan says as he unlocks my chains.

The blood starts to flow into my arms more freely. There's a partial relief from the intense ache, but they still feel so stiff. It's hard to imagine being able to move them, even after my bindings are completely off, and the anticipation increases the aching again.

His body hangs over me as he unwraps them from my wrists and arms. The red indentations left behind are raw, some with sores ground out by the metal. His breath is heavy and threatening. "Shit! Your arms are all marked up."

What did he expect? He runs his fingers through his hair. "What should we do? We can't postpone the rebirth."

I just want to be free, and clean. I'm sick of my rank smell. "It'll be better after I shower, hun, I can put makeup on them. It's not that bad."

The ache in my shoulders changes shape as he finishes unwrapping the chains and brings my arms down, completely freeing me. The sensation radiates up and threatens to travel through my body, taking it over. And I tremble as I inhabit my body again, letting myself feel sensation. Pain. So much pain.

I'm shaking, but I need to look like I'm under control. I need him to believe I'm his plaything. And playthings don't tremble—not unless they're told to. I steady myself and look up at Ryan and fake a bashful smile. "I must smell horrible, I'm just so embarrassed."

"There's no reason to be embarrassed. It's my fault, I should have let you wash up before. I just wasn't sure if I could trust you to do the right thing."

"Can you help me get to my feet so I can shower?"

My skin crawls as Ryan lifts me to my feet by my armpits. He holds me in place as I find my footing and figure out how to steady myself on my atrophied legs.

I'm so hungry, it's been ages since I've had anything to eat. If I could just eat something, anything, to gain my strength back. "Could I have something to eat before the...rebirthing? Or will there be food?"

Ryan shakes his head. "No, we need you pure." He points to the douching kit. "I need you to clean out your insides too."

He takes me to the bare clawfoot tub, it's disgusting inside. I desperately want to be clean, but it's hard to imagine it'll happen here. Ryan turns on the shower. The water is brown before it runs clear. Steam starts to rise as it heats up. The grime at the bottom of the tub loosens and slips down the open drain until it almost looks inviting.

My captor sits on the bed as he watches me shower, and I try to make it a show for him. It's not the first time I've performed for the benefit of a man that disgusts me. If I can get him to keep letting his guard down, I might have a chance to survive this.

I soap myself seductively as he watches, his hand squeezing his boner through his jeans. I run the loofah all around my curves, emphasizing my breasts, bending over and spreading myself open, lathering around my girldick. He's getting more excited.

I feel nauseous, but it's so nice to clean myself and feel the grime slide off my body and clean the sores on my arms. I shave my legs, they're clean and smooth again. I don't think I realized how dysphoric that was making me on top of everything else. The clashing sense of relief and revulsion makes me dizzy.

Ryan hands me a towel as I step out and dry myself off. He looks over to the makeup kit and lingerie. "Time to shine."

This might be my chance. Jane's knife is just under the nightstand. "Could you turn around while I make myself up and put this on? I want my look to be a surprise. To take your breath away."

He shakes his head. "Tempting, but I need to keep an eye on you."

Shit. I put on the lingerie; it's lacy and black with not much coverage down there. I'm completely hanging out of the large hole in the crotch, but it does have pretty good coverage on my chest. The top is like a typical bra, maybe I could hide the knife in there, if I can get to it. I open the makeup kit, it's an eyeshadow palette, foundation, contour, eyebrow pencil, mascara, eyeliner, some brushes and sponges, and a stick of red lipstick. My hands tremble as I sort through the items. I'm so weak, and I could easily drop these.

"Need you to drink this," Ryan says, holding a cup that's definitely roofied.

I spasm. The mascara bottle, foundation, and

sponge slip out of my hands and fall onto the floor. The mascara bottle rolls under the nightstand. Perfect. "Shit, sorry!"

I get down on my hands and knees and start to reach under the nightstand. I feel the knife! But I can sense him standing behind me, impatient.

I need to distract him, so I lift my ass up and sway seductively. This gets his attention, and he sets the glass of water down and puts his hands on me. I pretend to like his grabby touch, and softly moan. As he concentrates on squeezing my ass, I slip the knife into my bra, under my left boob, hoping that it won't be noticeable. I reach further back and grab the mascara bottle. "Got it!"

When will be the right moment to use the knife? How can I possibly escape? He's so strong, and there's a group of men in the next room—I don't know how many. I'm not even sure I can get out without a key, it's probably locked. And I'm so weak, I haven't eaten for days and my body aches so much.

I want to believe I can do this. But maybe this isn't the right moment. Am I even capable of hurting another person like this? Slicing into their flesh? Killing them? I've always considered myself a pacifist.

No. Girl, you have to defend yourself, you have to make it out alive. The knife is in your hands, and he's distracted. You may not have another chance, deal with the men outside when it comes to that. This is just like the time that guy wouldn't let you out of his car in Koreatown, and you had to brain him with your stiletto. You survived that and you can survive this.

    I pull the switchblade out from under my bra, spin around, and slash Ryan's neck.

CHAPTER 18

I bolt for the door, leaving behind Ryan holding the side of his neck where I cut him. He grunts in pain and shock. I wish I'd sliced his throat, but my aim wasn't perfect.

Bright lights sting my eyes in the parlor as I close the door to the master bedroom behind me. The room has been transformed, brightly lit. There's rows of folding metal chairs, and Ryan's creepy crew are sitting there—I don't recognize the pigman without his mask at first, but he's there with Dale and the rest. And there's other men—men I don't recognize, maybe a dozen of them. They're talking amongst themselves, while others are busy preparing for my "rebirth." Whatever bonkers shit that is.

They haven't noticed me yet, and I retract the

switchblade and place it into my bra. No, one of them has noticed me. It's a man I don't recognize operating a large camera attached to a laptop. He doesn't alert anyone else, but he rushes to do something on the computer. Are they recording this? Live streaming it?

There's a makeshift stage to the right of me, not raised but marked out by fake hardwood tiles on the floor. Center stage is a bed with a red comforter and pink sheets, and a stuffed pink headboard with an ornate gold frame. Shackles hang from the headboard, clearly meant for me. Next to it is another row of six folding chairs, populated by the realistic trans sex dolls I'd seen the men playing with when I was first dragged up here. They're all wearing matching lingerie, the same as mine, with their perfectly rendered outies hanging out of the crotch-holes.

But the stark light shows me there's something off about them, they don't look like the silicone sex dolls I've seen online or in Dale's bedroom. They're too realistic, too uncanny, but at the same time have the imperfections of a DIY project. Their skin has a gloss to it, but it looks kind of…dry. Not the fake suppleness of silicon. It reminds me of the dead bodies I saw in an anatomy exhibit that were preserved with some sort of plastic.

It can't be. Were these once women?

I recognize one of them! It's Jane's friend. She's still wearing that high ponytail, but her face is frozen in an unnatural smile. My stomach lurches, it's like they've had the worst face lifts and work done that I've ever seen. My head swims and my gaze floats back to the men. They want to turn me into a preserved corpse-doll!

They've noticed me, and are staring with mild confusion, wondering if the show has already begun. What's behind them, in the back of the room, comes into focus now, the plastic curtains are open, revealing the inside of the separated "clean" area. It looks a little like a makeshift laboratory or operating room. Two men in white paper suits and safety goggles are making preparations. They stand next to a vat full of some sort of bubbling chemical with a familiar smell. In the corner is a small pile of human body parts, some must be Jane's, and there's a corpse of a woman I don't recognize, her arms and legs no longer attached to her body. It's a human-doll workshop. I dry heave—there's nothing in my stomach to throw up.

My reaction starts to tip off the men that something is off-plan. Get a hold of yourself, girl. You need to escape. Dale looks at me and blurts out, "Where's Ryan?"

As if on cue, Ryan bursts out of the bedroom in a

rage, causing the swinging door to slam loudly against the wall. Tied tight around his neck is a white cloth, stained with blood on the side. He grunts and points at me and gestures to the rest of them to restrain me. Stun guns crackle as two huge men walk toward me, along with some of the others in Ryan's crew. A second camera man closes in too, getting a better shot of the scene beginning to form.

"Don't leave any marks," Ryan says, in a strained voice. "We need her untouched."

I pull out Jane's knife from my bra and release the blade. Me and our little knife against a secret club of serial-killer chasers. The odds are shit.

My throat is dry, I swallow. Gripping Jane's knife tighter, I remember what she told me. Even if they take you, even if they kill you, don't give them what they want. I'm a goddess? I have the perfect body? Not anymore.

I pull on my dick, making the flaccid member taught—I never cared for this thing anyway—and cut it in half. Blood runs down my arm as I hold my severed genital in my hand and scream in pain and rage. They can kill me, but I will never give them what they want.

The men freeze in place, consumed by shock, all of the color in their faces has dropped into their guts. Ryan is the first one to break the silence. "No! NO! What have you done, you fucking cunt!"

Dale screams like a jet engine, and his scream sets off a shockwave of wails from the others. It's only a moment before all of the men in the room are howling and screaming, holding their heads, dropping to their knees, hyperventilating. I've broken something inside them.

The hippy guy tears his hair out, one uses his stun gun on his own crotch, and the pigman slams a folding metal chair to the ground violently. He turns the violence to his own head, blood spilling from a growing gash from the metal striking his face. One of the men in clean suits jumps into the chemical bath, splashing around and screeching as it evaporates the moisture in his body. They are all losing their shit. I drop the knife and the piece of me in shock, overwhelmed by the torrent of self-harm.

A series of scream-yells grows until it's louder than the rest. It's coming from Ryan who's on his knees. His large fingers are deep into his eye sockets. He plucks his eyeballs out as bright red blood runs down like an impossible flood of tears. He squeezes around them, crushing them into pulp that slips out of trembling palms.

I'm getting lightheaded, I need to stop my own bleeding. The dolls stare at me with their false eyes as I stumble over to the bed and pull off a pillowcase, bunching it up and pressing it between my legs. They deserved better.

Pain from my groin is starting to grow as I limp through the room toward the elevator, through the chaos of screaming, sniveling, raging unhinged men, consumed by the wreckage of their perfect fantasy ruined.

CHAPTER 19

My door is unlocked, and I stumble into my apartment. Kierra is on the couch, hair and mascara a mess, and covered in popcorn crumbs while watching some trashy reality TV show. My slight regret about giving her a spare key dissolves. Her jaw drops, and she jumps to her feet when she sees me. "Lenora! I knew it!"

"Kierra, thank god." We embrace, it hurts, but the warmth of my best friend is healing.

Fresh tears smudge her mascara even more. "Babe, we've been looking for you, we put up flyers all the way to Santa Monica. And I've been posting on our socials non-stop in hopes a fan spotted you. I knew those texts weren't you, I knew you wouldn't skip out on us like that."

My voice is weak, "Thanks. Your face is a mess."

She laughs until she notices my condition. "You're hurt! Oh my god, you're bleeding! We gotta get you to a hospital."

"Yea, but can we get a fucking veggie burger first?"

Kierra helps me throw on a t-shirt and sweatpants over my lingerie and drives me to the ER. She has the better judgment for once, and we don't stop for food on the way, but her driving is panicked. The ER waiting room is packed, and I guess bleeding out from your crotch isn't a reason to be seen right away. The receptionist is cold when Kierra advocates on my behalf, failing to get me to the front of the line. How will I afford this? I don't have insurance. I don't even have money.

In a hushed voice, I tell Kierra what happened to me through tears, keeping my volume low so the others in the waiting room won't think I'm crazy. I can barely get it out, and reliving the incident puts me back to the apartment. I'm shaking, and she holds me, sharing my tears. She doesn't respond but her eyes and embrace tell me she believes every word. I don't know if anyone else will except for Max. It barely even feels real to me.

A man who's been talking to himself for the past 20 minutes says, "Fucking tranny cut its dick off," and snorts. I swear one of the hospital staff is holding back laughter at that. After half an hour, I'm brought to another room for the rest of my intake. They send me to surgery as soon as they realize the extent of my injury.

 I lay in the hospital bed, alone in my new room, and the slightly scratchy sheets are a greater comfort than I could have ever imagined. A plastic cup of applesauce sits on the tray. My stomach growls. I'm still sore and groggy from the surgery—there was nothing to reattach, and I definitely didn't want penile reconstruction. I don't exactly understand what they did, but I guess they are holding it together until I can get vaginoplasty. The surgeon said that's still an option even though my results may not be ideal. Not how I imagined getting bottom surgery, but okay.

 When I told the doctor that it was an accident, she didn't push back but she mentioned the hospital has resources. Maybe she meant a social worker or something? I don't want to talk. How would I explain it to a stranger?

 And if I told someone what happened, would the cops get involved? Would they even believe me? Would they even care if they did? Doubtful.

 But if there's any chance that those men could hurt more girls… I need to say something. I'll make something up that sounds more believable, just something that will get them to go to the presidential suite, and they can piece together the rest. I'll say something. I'll figure it out. I just need a little rest first.

Morning visiting hours are finally here, and Kierra and Max are let in to keep me company. They give me gentle hugs, careful to avoid unhooking my IV. Kierra stole me a half dozen gossip magazines from the waiting room, and Max has a veggie burger and fries for me.

Max immediately goes into "fix it" mode, which has annoyed me in the past, but the kindness of it fills my heart and makes me smile.

"Are you in pain?"

"Are you cold?"

"Do you need water?"

I nod, and they bring me a Styrofoam cup of water and disappear to find a nurse to get me more blankets and meds.

"Those disgusting pieces of shit can't get away with this," Max says, containing their anger so it doesn't feel threatening. "We have to do something."

Fear rushes into my body, and I'm looking through the peephole again at Jane's bloody, mangled face, held up by Ryan for me to see. The maw of his wolf mask is stained with blood, a strand of her messed up hair lies across its realistic teeth. The flashback dissipates with a violent shake of my head. "Max, please, I don't want to think about it. I need to rest."

They kiss me on the forehead, and the last traces of panic melt out of my body. "I'm sorry, love. We're here. He can't hurt you anymore."

My friends sit with me in silence for the next hour as I lay back in the hospital bed, the moment punctuated by the whirring and beeping of machines and the rhythm of doctors and nurses coming in and out. I'm so grateful to be with people who love me. To just be.

There's commotion from down the hall, a crashing of medical equipment and the scream of a nurse, and I hear a panicked voice. "You can't be in here!"

Ryan bursts through my hospital room door. He's covered in blood and grime, wearing sunglasses over his bleeding eyes. His manic, blood-stained grimace stretches across his face like a joker, and veins bulge from his neck and biceps. His fists are tight and red. Kierra, Max, and I scream in surprise and terror.

Two staff members pull him from behind, and his sunglasses clatter to the floor revealing his empty bleeding sockets where his eyes once were. How did he find me? How?

He pushes toward me, reaching his arms out, knocking my tray of food across the room. I jump back, causing searing pain in my wound, and Max and Kierra pounce on him. Something flies out of his hand and bounces onto the bed.

More hospital staff pour in, and they pin my attacker to the ground. He pants, and I hold my breath. His panting turns into wheezing and finally a strange gurgling until he's still and silent on the ground with an amused grin frozen on his face.

"He's dead," someone says.

I sob with relief, and then notice what he dropped. At the foot of the bed lies my flaccid flesh.

EPILOGUE

...and that's why he drives a 2026 Ford Summit Crusher: because the size of your truck does matter...

...Next tonight, a massive global outbreak of violent self-harm episodes by young men is baffling experts. Warning: the images just in may not be suitable for sensitive viewers. Look at this harrowing video, a close up shot of one of the victims taken minutes after disaster struck. He mercilessly slit his own throat with a kitchen knife, just gruesome. And here's another victim who stuck his hand in a blender, a terrifying display of pure insanity. Channel 4's Wanda Weiss live from Washington D.C. has the details...

Sarah, thousands of men committed extreme acts of self-harm early Wednesday morning, with The FBI and *international authorities reporting a cumulative one thousand dead and two thousand injured—some in critical condition. Authorities say they don't yet know the cause of the disaster, but that most of the men's bodies were found at home, some mutilated beyond all recognition.*

Wanda, did they say anything about the intriguing rumors online that these men had all visited the same encrypted website on the dark web, shortly before their episode? And there's a video with some sort of hypnotic or horrifying imagery that influenced them to commit these tragic acts?

Terrifying, but a spokesperson for the FBI said that these claims are baseless, and to stay calm.

But what caused this? Have they found any connection between the men at all?

Experts are pointing to this being a severe anomaly. An unusual number of unconnected, simultaneous freak-accidents, a grim reminder of the epidemic of male loneliness. It's a growing problem that's been plaguing America and countries around the world, affecting millions of men of all ages. And we have Channel Four's Richard Bailey with a special report on this heartbreaking modern condition...

...Men. Who is today's man? Is there still a place for men in our woke, modern society? And why are

millions of men shunned every day instead of being supported? I'm Dick Bailey, with tonight's special report, No Man Should Be an Island: The Truth About Male Loneliness in the Twenty-first Century...

ACKNOWLEDGEMENTS

So many have helped and enriched us in our lives and creative journeys, and we appreciate you all, but we'd like to call out a few people who have particularly impacted us in a positive way.

Mariah would like to acknowledge her loving mother and four supportive brothers.

Eve would like to acknowledge her parents, brothers, and wife for loving, supporting, believing in, and inspiring her. She'd like to thank Beth Stephens and Annie Sprinkle for their love and mentorship in college, and showing her that being her true self was possible. She'd also like to thank Lucas Mangum and Laurel Hightower who were early believers and supporters of her work, and continue to be generous friends and cohorts.

We'd both like to thank Ben Sinclair and Laurel Hightower who read early versions of the *Chasers* manuscript and provided valuable feedback and encouragement.

We'd also like to thank our publisher Eddie at Unnerving for his belief in our story, and his patience, care, and hard work to make this book the best it can be for our readers. His commitment and ingenuity in creating vehicles to launch and support marginalized writers is a boon to the horror fiction community.

And finally, we'd like to acknowledge the contributions of black trans women to the LGBT community and culture.

www.ingramcontent.com/pod-product-compliance
Lightning Source LLC
LaVergne TN
LVHW012018200225
803813LV00007B/116